MW01126920

Darkness Descends on Princeton

A 1930's murder mystery

Jeff Jacobs

Copyright © 2014 Jeff Jacobs

All rights reserved.

ISBN-13: 978-1463654597
ISBN-10: 1463654596

Special thanks!

Most beautifully edited
by
Judy Buckley-Jacobs

Scathingly brilliant cover art
by
Kate Gabrielle

Epic support
from
Kyle Jacobs

Dedicated to the memory of my parents,
Gordon and Eve Jacobs

READING INSTRUCTIONS

Read this story as if you're watching a murder mystery movie from the 1930's, with all of the iconic supporting character actors included.

Grab the popcorn.

The feature presentation is about to begin.

1

It all started with a body on the floor at a home in Princeton, New Jersey. Actually, it started a little before that.

It was a brisk autumn day in 1939. The leaves were starting to turn to reds and yellows on Bayard Lane and through the glass French doors at one home you could see the daily routine of piano lessons in progress. Halfway through Chopin's Sonata No. 2 the telephone rang. Professor Menjou, disturbed by the interruption, slammed his palm on the piano. "Eve, please break while I attend to this," he said while heading to the far end of the room to answer the call.

Eve lightly rested her hands over the keys and stared at her reflection in the huge silver candelabra that sat upon the grand piano in front of her. "I need to do something with this hair," she thought, "it just doesn't go well with this dress." She pushed her curly brown hair up off her shoulders to see what a shorter cut might look like.

"This is a piano lesson not a hair salon, Miss Krell." The professor had finished his call and was back to his dictatorial style of teaching. "Now, from the beginning...and remember, the keys are there to be pressed, not dusted." He was referring to Eve's soft touch in playing that sometimes resulted in a scarcity of sound being emitted from the piano. She started again, trying hard to concentrate on her teacher's advice. She listened closely for a murmur of disapproval which would sometimes rise to an awkward grunt if she hit a wrong key. Strangely she heard nothing of that sort, only the distracting sound of Professor Menjou pacing around the room, which was especially more disturbing because it was so out of character.

Originally it was the professor's habit of standing as rigid as a statue facing a blank wall while listening to her that made her uneasy. After months of lessons, though, she had adjusted to that style of behavior, so this abrupt change made her feel as if a roomful of people were watching her. She could feel herself losing concentration on the piece she was supposed to be playing. She was gritting her teeth trying hard to correctly hit each key. Then the phone rang again. Again she was told to break and the professor hurried over to the phone.

Thinking it was the previous call that had caused the professor's anguish, Eve strained to listen this time. She heard him say something like "are you sure they know?" in a very alarmed manner. But then he turned his head slightly toward Eve and, realizing that she was listening, changed his tone, "Look, dear, we can discuss it over some cocktails tonight." His new attitude was light and cheerful. "Maybe we can take in a picture after dinner...Fine...I'll see you tonight." He hung up the phone and apologized to Eve for the interruptions.

"Continue," he said. She began playing again, from the first note, but she could again detect the uneasiness in the professor's movements. She did not know how she would make it through the complete lesson. Then, in quick succession, she heard a loud bang, a groaning sound, and something falling. She turned in time to see the professor crumpling to the floor.

Startled, she jumped up from her seat, causing the candelabra to fall onto the keys as she bumped the piano. She caught the candelabra at the same time her piano bench fell backward to the ground. She ran over to the professor, absent-mindedly placing the candelabra on the floor next to him.

"Professor! Are you okay?" she asked.

He simply rolled his eyes at the question before losing consciousness. It was then that she noticed his white shirt beneath his open jacket. It was covered in blood.

2

Thoughts crowded her mind: He's been shot! How? Who? There's no one here. Is he dead?

She nudged him. "Professor? Professor?"

There was no response. Was he dead? She grabbed his wrist to feel for a pulse. She was shaking so badly that she couldn't hold his hand steady. Calm down, she told herself, calm down. There was no pulse. He was dead...and what if the killer was still in the room. She stayed crouched next to the body with her head tilted toward her dead piano teacher. Her eyes slowly scanned the room for signs of an intruder. A murmuring breeze from outside was the only noise. Inside the room it was eerily quiet.

She looked toward a couch in the far corner of the room. Nothing. But could someone be hiding behind it? She couldn't tell. The doorway into the library was open and the corridor seemed empty. Late day shadows kept moving across the space and her eyes paused there, concentrating, looking for any movements. Her heart froze when she thought she saw fingers curled around the frame of the doorway. She stared hard at the spot but it was nothing. Her eyes moved on. Lamps, chairs, tables - helped by the playful shadows – all seemed partners in hiding a killer.

She turned slightly to the right to scan the next area of the room, focusing on an area between the professor's favorite high back chair and a small table that held a precariously high stack of hard cover books. There, the two pieces of furniture sat in front of a ceiling-to-floor curtain that masked a huge window overlooking the side of the home. Eve froze when the folds in the curtains moved slightly. When they moved again she thought she saw, in the folds and shadows, the outline of a person. She waited for movement again and when it came and seemed to be in concert with the outdoor breeze, she dismissed it as another false alarm. But then her eyes peered down to floor level. In the miniscule space between the bottom of the curtains and the floor she could see two shoes - men's shoes.

"I am either the only witness," she thought, "or the next victim." Again, she willed herself to stay calm. She looked to the other end of the room where the French doors to the back patio were partly open. In one quick movement, she grabbed the candelabra sitting next to the body, stood up and with all her might hurled it at the figure in the curtains. Somehow it made it far enough to land where the man's knees must have been. She heard an awful deep groan and the sound of breaking glass as the murderer fell backward through the window.

Eve didn't get to see the results of her handiwork, though. As soon as the candelabra was on its way, she was on her way out of the French doors. She hopped over the thorny shrubbery that bordered the patio and raced to her car with only the crinkling sound of dried leaves on the ground following her. After fumbling with the keys to her father's 1937 Hudson she got it started and shoved it in gear. As she let go of the clutch, the car lurched backward into the oak tree directly behind her. She noisily jerked the reluctant gear into drive and the car lunged forward, brushed by a row of blooming mums, hopped over the curb and headed down Bayard Lane. She headed straight for the police station, which was just a few minutes away on Nassau Street. Professor Menjou – dead! Eve's mind wandered. He hadn't been the friendliest piano teacher in the world, well, maybe the meanest would be a better description. Those sarcastic remarks: "Take off your winter mittens and play that again!" He could be very demeaning. But dead! What could he have done to deserve that. And now the murderer would be gone and it was too late for poor Professor Menjou.

Eve was riding right on the tail of old Charlie Grapewin in his Model T. He was chugging along at a snail's pace and right in the middle of the road, too. She beeped and tried to pass but there was no way Charlie would move. And, as their cars got closer to downtown, more traffic clogged the roads. She had almost come to a stop when she saw the offices of the local newspaper, The Princeton Topic. "Gordon! He must be working!" She thought of her boyfriend of just going on eight months. She could get his help and call the police from their office. She pulled off the road and parked right in front of the small storefront office. As she burst through the front door, she bumped into and was nearly bowled over by Grant Mitchell, the short stocky publisher, editor and manager of the paper. Barely noticing her, he continued on through the open door into his office. Eve yelled, "Where's Gordon?" interrupting Spring Byington, the secretary, who was on the phone and filing her nails at the same time.

"Excuse me, Madge," Spring said to the person on the phone, "I have someone here, so I'm going to have to go. I'll call you later… but you did say that was three eggs beaten slightly, then add the paprik…"

Eve interrupted again. "Sorry, Spring, this is an

emergency. Is Gordon here?"

Spring held the phone down, looked toward the open door to Mr. Mitchell's office and whispered to Eve, "He's not here yet."

Like a bolt, Mr. Mitchell was at his doorway. "Not here? Not here, Miss Byington? For the last two hours every time I've asked for him you've told me he has been in the bathroom! A bad piece of meat on his sandwich for lunch, you said. He just doesn't have a strong stomach, you said. He had to take some bromide tablets, you said. And now, now you say he is not here!" Mr. Mitchell's face was turning red and what little gray hair he had (that was neatly combed over his head) now seemed to be popping up in all different directions to reflect his irritation.

"He has only been working here three months, and, to tell you the truth, Miss Byington, I don't think he's been WORKING HERE more than three days!" He turned around, went back into his office and slammed the door.

Eve and Spring looked at each other with blank stares. The door opened again and Mitchell took one step out.

"And furthermore – Gordon is fired!!" And the door slammed closed again.

"Oh, geez. This is all my fault," Eve said, tears peeking out of her eyes. "I didn't mean to get him in trouble."

"Now, now. Don't even think that way, Eve. It's not your fault at all. Mr. Mitchell has just had a bad day and he has not been in a very good mood at…." The door opened again.

"What do you mean 'a bad mood'? I am NOT in a bad mood. I'm just running this stupid newspaper." He extended both arms out to show the all-encompassing immenseness of the 800 square foot office. "And what in

God's name do you want?" His eyes pierced Eve with the demand for an immediate response.

Eve whispered weakly, "Professor Menjou has been murdered," and then fell to the floor in a faint.

3

The rumble, bumps and screeches of the trolley headed down Mercer Street did nothing to disrupt the concentration of one passenger. Leaning forward in a window seat, Gordon Radits was lost in the open book on his lap, his thick black hair and dark eyes making him look more like a university student totally engulfed in the contents, as if preparing for an upcoming exam. The trolley stopped and started, commuters added and subtracted and this one rider oblivious to it all. Even when a new arrival sat on the bench seat next to him, slightly jostling him, Gordon didn't lose his focus.

"What is it that you are reading?" an inquisitive voice asked.

"Well, H.G. Wells," Gordon replied without looking up.

"Which one?" the persistent voice asked. "He has written many books."

"The Shape of…" Gordon started to reply as this time he looked up and then recognized his fellow traveler. "Oh, Professor Einstein! How are you today?"

"Oh, a little bit chilly. I think the weather is starting to turn. I did not come out prepared for the cold." Einstein was wearing a gray cardigan sweater that had somehow lost the middle of the five buttons. He looked a bit disheveled, but that was the way Gordon always thought of him. "Yes," he continued, "Mr. Wells is a very interesting man. Very prolific. The Shape of Things to Come. Good, so far?"

"It's great, professor. I can't put it down… as you can see."

"So, are you very interested in the future? As a subject?"

"Yes. Definitely."

"Gordon, have you read Wells' essays on the World Brain?"

Gordon quickly replied, "Is that all about YOU, Professor?"

Einstein broke into a grin, chuckled and said, "Very good. You have just been complimentary and humorous at the same time. It is quite an accomplishment."

"Thanks, Professor." Gordon beamed. Any accolades from Einstein were huge ego boosters.

"If you get the opportunity, look for the World Brain. It's Wells' idea of the future of shared knowledge and how it will improve our world. But, let me actually interrupt your reading for one little mathematics exercise." Einstein turned more directly in Gordon's direction.

"Sure, Professor." Gordon was a bit puzzled by this new direction the conversation was taking.

Einstein began, "Say you have a fixed point. As a moving object approaches that fixed point, the distance between the object and the fixed point gets smaller – decreases. And when you reach the fixed point, there is nothing between the object and the fixed point. But, and this is the most important part of this exercise, if the distance between the object and the fixed point starts and increases, it means that… well, it means that you have missed your stop."

Einstein stopped there, his eyes looking directly at

Gordon and then moving to the window where Gordon's eyes joined his. The trolley was on Nassau Street. Gordon had gone two stops past The Topic office. He hurriedly thanked the Professor as he grabbed his book and a folder on the seat and sprinted to get off the trolley. Einstein laughed to himself quietly, as did a short balding man sitting across the aisle who had got on the trolley the same time Einstein did. The man had listened to the recent conversation, kept a safe distance and then got off and followed Einstein into Firestone Library.

4

Gordon zigzagged through traffic and headed back toward The Topic office. Missing his stop made him realize that he was also missing the deadline for his story on the Princeton-Yale football game. As The Topic's lone sports reporter, the whole sports section of the publication was dependent on him. He could hear Mr. Mitchell's reaction in his head: "Where have you been? Don't you know I have a newspaper to get out?" He knew it would probably be nice if he didn't always stop the presses – literally.

He couldn't help it, though, if he wanted to write about more than just sports. He was always trying to work in other stories, things that were new and relevant, or at least things to make readers think. And always the same exasperated response from Mitchell: "I pay you to write sports. S-P-O-R-T-S!"

Everyone told him he was a good writer, and luckily, Gordon had the head news writer, Franchot Tone, on his side. Tone, tall and distinguished, would give his overwrought boss a sly smile and say, "C'mon, Chief, this is a great piece Gordon's written. Do you know what this will do for circulation? Boom! It'll take it through the ceiling!" Mitchell would throw up his hands in resignation. "Go ahead. Put it in. What do I care? I only own the darn newspaper!" And as Tone patted him on the back in thanks, Mitchell stormed off to his office and slammed the door behind him. Only rarely, like Gordon's story about the first jet flight back in August and what it portended for the future of flying, did Mitchell actually compliment him. Of course, a passing mumbling of, "Nice job on that story," was the extent of the praise, but Gordon was more than grateful for these small miracles.

Not stopping to catch his breath, Gordon ran straight down Nassau Street toward The Topic building. As he approached, he could see Eve's car parked more haphazardly than usual in front of the door. Accustomed to her less than perfect driving skills, his only thought was, "Swell! Eve's here to see me." He arrived at exactly the same moment as a screeching police car pulled up to the paper's front door.

Two men emerged from the car. The driver was Officer Nat Pendleton, a husky ex-boxer who did not seem bright enough to drive a car let alone solve a crime. In fact, at that moment, he was having problems closing his car door. He had hopped out of the car and flung the door closed, but it popped back open. He slammed it again with the same result. Meanwhile, the other passenger had emerged and was staring at Pendleton, arms positioned on his hips. Detective Sergeant James Gleason was a wiry Irishman with a hardnosed Brooklyn accent. He rarely had patience for such trivial nonsense.

"Pendleton! Can it!" he barked. "We'll fix that door when we fix your empty skull. Now leave it and let's go."

They reached the entrance just as Gordon was grabbing the door knob.

"Out of the way. Princeton Police Department," Gleason bellowed as he butted in front of Gordon to enter the office. The two policemen stopped inside the doorway to survey the situation. Gordon stepped forward, not knowing what was going on. His eyes scanned the room until he could see between Gleason and Pendleton. There, lying on the floor, was Eve.

"Out of the way. That's my girl!" he yelled as he shoved between them and ran to her.

5

Spring Byington was still holding the smelling salts under Eve's nose while Mitchell was bringing a wet towel over from the sink. Eve was just regaining consciousness.

"What happened, Eve, honey? Are you alright?" Gordon knelt down beside her. The two policemen also crouched down around her.

"Silly me," Eve started, "I think everything that happened just hit me all at once. I just remember getting light-headed… and then everything went dark."

Spring took over for her. "Eve must have been at her piano lesson when Professor Menjou was murdered."

"Murdered? Who would kill Professor Menjou?" Gordon asked. "Eve, are you alright?"

"Of course she's alright," Officer Pendleton broke in. "She's here, ain't she?" Everyone shot him a dirty look. Sergeant Gleason cut in, "We got a call about gunshots and sent a couple of men over to the Menjou home right away. There's a call out for any suspicious characters in the area. Everything's under control and we'll have this case solved in a jiffy." He continued, "As soon as you feel up to it, Miss Krell, we'll take a ride over to the Menjou place and try to sort things out."

Eve nodded and started to sit up. Gordon helped her over to Spring's desk and eased her into the chair. "Someone get a pillow for her head," he requested.

"A pillow? We don't have any pillows in a newspaper office," Mitchell growled.

"Sure we do, Chief," Gordon said, "there's the one you keep in the bottom drawer of your desk for when you take a nap at work."

"I do not take naps at work," he announced, turning red and fumbling for words. "That pillow is for when I'm working into the wee hours of the morning waiting for you to meet yesterday's deadlines." He continued, "And by the way, where is that story that was supposed to be here two hours ago? I have a good mind to fire you, Radits."

While this ranting was going on, Spring had gone into his office and returned with a tan rectangular pillow. She gently placed it behind Eve's head. Gleason broke the short silence. "Mr. Mitchell, your story is going to have to wait a bit. We've got a murder to solve."

Everything settled down for a while as Eve got her bearings and recounted the events to the assembled group. Spring provided tea and coffee. Grant Mitchell controlled his smoldering irritation by pacing up and down and then headed into his office to take some pills. When Eve quietly stated, "I think I'm ready," she and Gordon climbed into her car, Gordon taking the wheel. Gleason and Pendleton led the way in their police car, and one by one they pulled up to the stately home on Bayard Lane that was now blockaded by police barriers.

They entered by way of the front door, which led to a

narrow hallway with rooms branching out on both sides. Midway through the length of the house, they could either go up a circular flight of stairs to the bedrooms or they could make a left into the library, which had also served as the location for piano lessons, and… the scene of the crime.

There were two officers leaning against the French doors looking out into the yard. In the room, two men were preparing to remove the sheet-covered body from the scene. The coroner, a short man with a big round face and a crooked bow-tie, was Dr. Eric Blore. He was busy on the telephone and put his hand up to Sergeant Gleason to indicate he would be with him shortly.

"No," Blore insisted to the other party on the phone, "the cause of death was a bullet wound through the right ventricle and the aorta. No. I said 'aorta' not hayorta. A… A… A as in apple. A-P-P-L-E. No. Not D. I said P. P as in pumpkin. P-U-M-P-K-I-N. No, no. Not N. M. M as in mahogany. M as in… oh just forget it. Just put down that he was killed at 6:05 p.m. and I'll fill in the rest when I get back. No. Killed. K-I-L…. Oh, goodbye!" He slammed down the phone and rolled his eyes.

Sergeant Gleason took no chances that Blore would be sidetracked again. "A bullet to the heart, eh?"

"That is correct."

"Anything else you can tell me?"

"He was shot at relatively short range – maybe close to or just under ten feet. I'll know more after we get him back to the lab." Blore clasped his bag closed and signaled the two men to proceed with the body. "You can call me tomorrow afternoon, Sergeant," he said, passing Gleason on his way out.

"I'll call you first thing in the morning, Doc," Gleason replied, trying not so subtly to push Blore for earlier results.

"Well, I won't be there first thing in the morning, so if one of the dead bodies answers the phone, just leave a message and I'll get back to you… TOMORROW… AFTERNOON." He tipped his hat to Eve and left.

6

The rest of them filed into the room. Gordon held onto Eve as she tentatively moved past the piano. With the body gone, only some blood stains on the floor gave a hint at what had occurred. They went over toward the window where Eve had thrown the candelabra. The curtains were barely hanging - the man grasping at them as he fell backward had snapped the heavy wooden rod holding them from the top and they now drooped lazily to one side. Gordon parted the thick white curtains to reveal shattered glass scattered across the lawn. Some depressed branches on a small bush marked the spot right underneath the windowsill where the man had landed. Whoever fell through the window apparently was able to escape unharmed as there was no sign of blood.

They turned their attention back inside the room. The sergeant asked Eve to go to where she was at the time of the murder. She went to the piano and neatly folding her skirt, sat on the now upright sturdy wooden piano bench.

"If it doesn't upset you too much, just go through the events…." Gleason was interrupted as Pendleton nudged him.

"We got the missus. They're bringing her in the house now."

"Does she know what happened?" Gordon asked.

Pendleton scratched his head. "Apparently, she already…." He was cut short as Officer O'Leary led the sobbing woman into the room. A very formal woman with short brown hair and thin features, her reddened face was partially covered by a white lace handkerchief that was soaked with tears and covered with mascara.

"Poor Mrs. Menj…." Eve began to cry and set off toward her. But the distressed woman abruptly lifted her head and pointed her right hand directly at Eve.

"That's her. She's the one. She murdered my husband."

7

Eve stopped in her tracks. "What! What are you saying?"

"You killed him. Confess now, Eve. You can't get away with it," Mrs. Menjou said. "Sergeant Gleason, you must arrest this woman."

A confused Sergeant Gleason stepped between the two women. "You're saying that Eve Krell – this woman, right here – shot and killed your husband, Adolph Menjou?"

"That is correct," she replied.

"Did you see this murder?"

"Not exactly. But…."

"Then how do you know she's guilty?"

Mrs. Menjou looked at Sergeant Gleason and Officer Pendleton and would no longer look in Eve's direction. "I was upstairs," she stated through sobs. "I was in the bath. I could hear the piano being played. Then it stopped for a short period, then it started again. Then it stopped and I heard shouting – a young woman's voice – angry and loud. It kept on. I got out of the bath and threw on some clothes. As I ran to the steps, she was still shouting. Then I heard a sound – a gunshot. I started to run down the stairs, but I thought I heard her coming toward the stairs so I ran back to our bedroom and tried to climb out the window and down the trellis. I fell and cut my head." She removed her red embroidered hat to reveal a bandage over her right ear. "I must have lost consciousness," she continued, "because when I came to it was visibly darker out. I did not want to go back into the house. I was terrified that this… woman… would still be there. I went across our yard to our neighbor, Mrs. Dumont. Margaret helped me in and bandaged my wound while I called the police." She turned away, putting her forearm up over her eyes. "Please… just take this woman out of my sight…." She went over to the high back chair, slumped down into it and dabbed her red eyes with the white handkerchief.

"It's not true!" Eve screamed. "None of this is true! I don't know why you're doing this."

Gleason stepped in front of her and placed his hand up as if to cover her mouth. "Eve, I'm sorry. But right now shouting isn't going to get us anywhere."

Eve looked around for support from Gordon, but he was nowhere to be found.

"Look, Eve," Sergeant Gleason continued, "I'm very sorry but I have no choice. I'll have to take you in on suspicion of murdering Adolph Menjou." He turned to Pendleton, who was leaning against the piano. "Take Miss Krell down to the station." He pulled out a pocket watch from inside his suit coat pocket, checked the time and then said, "I'll finish up here and have O'Leary bring me back."

Pendleton went over to lead Eve to the police car. She was in a daze, unable to grasp the accusation against her, while at the same time being deeply bothered by Gordon's disappearance. She looked one more time at Mrs. Menjou before being taken away. She had known the Professor's wife for years, ever since she had begun piano lessons as a teenager. Mrs. Menjou had always been a bit reserved in her demeanor, but Eve always thought they liked each other. A cup of ice cold lemonade in the summer or a hot cup of tea in the winter, a little conversation and a heartfelt interest in what was going on in Eve's life had always made her feel welcome in their home. How the distraught wife could believe that Eve was the murderer was hard to fathom. How she could have made up such a preposterous story was beyond comprehension.

Pendleton lightly tapped Eve's shoulder. "Sorry, miss. We gotta' go." Eve nodded and followed him out the door. It was pitch black outside except for secondary light coming from the house and a dim glow from a street lamp. Pendleton helped Eve into the car and then got in the driver's seat. Almost perfectly synchronized with the starting of the engine, a figure dashed out of the bushes from the passenger side of the car and hurled a bunch of garden tools toward the car. As shovels, a hoe and a big wide rake bounced onto the hood and windshield of the car, the figure dashed off to the left and out of sight.

"STOP!" Pendleton yelled. "This is the police!" He turned to Eve and said, "You stay right here where you are." He was out of the car in a flash and ran around the front of the house. As soon as Pendleton was out of sight, Gordon popped out of the bushes and slid into the driver's seat.

"Are you alright?" he said to Eve while slamming his foot down on the accelerator.

She stuttered, trying to speak while the car lunged

forward. "Where were you? Wait… we can't just take this police car… I'm under arrest… where are we going?... I'm… I'm… I'll be a fugitive. They'll think I'm guilty." She was frantically spitting out her every thought as the car zoomed down Bayard Lane and made a quick turn down a side street. "Don't you know how much trouble you're getting me in?" she shouted at him.

"You're being accused of murder… you're already in trouble," he retorted.

"Well, then how much MORE trouble you're getting me in…."

He suddenly made a sharp turn and pulled to a dead stop at the end of a dark narrow alleyway. He shut off the car and turned to Eve. "Look, we have to act fast. We don't have time to bicker. Here's what we know. Mrs. Menjou has made up a story of being there and hearing you kill her husband…."

"Wait. How do you know she wasn't…."

"Don't interrupt. We don't have time. I'll fill you in later. Let's just say when I heard her accusing you and the story she told I snuck out the patio doors and climbed up the trellis to the second floor. I checked her bathroom. The tub was completely dry – not possible if she had taken a bath. No signs at all that she had even recently used that room. No wet towels, anything. Plus I had seen her earlier today in town and she was wearing the same red dress she was wearing just now. If you take a bath, you do not put your same clothes back on. But enough about that. Right now, if the police have you, you're stuck. Mrs. Menjou is one of the most highly regarded people in the community. Your word against hers. No chance. We have to figure this thing out first. Now, just let me finish. First, I'm going to get you to a safe place where they can't find you. This is a police car so it's not like we can drive around and be inconspicuous. We're going to get out of the car, then just follow me and be quiet." They climbed out of the police car and crossed through the alley to a small yard full of thickets and brush. They zigzagged through the yard like it was a corn maze and exited at what turned out to be the rear door of The Topic. "I know my shortcuts," Gordon whispered proudly. "Stay here a second."

He poked himself halfway into the back door and then slid all the way in. The time he was gone seemed like an eternity to Eve but she was startled when seconds later, he quietly popped back out. "I've arranged everything. Spring is going to be distracting Mr. Mitchell. You go through this door and right down the stairs to your right."

"Not the dungeon…."

"Yes. THE dungeon."

"But I've never been down there."

"You'll love it," Gordon shot back. The dungeon was what they called the cellar of The Topic building. It was where the printing press was located – a big ancient hulk of a machine that rattled, snorted and shook the whole building to the point where visitors feared to tread anywhere near it.

"Eve, we don't have much time. Go now. I have to go take care of a couple of things and then I'll be back for you." He peeked in to make sure the coast was clear and then he gave her a quick kiss before shoving her through the doorway. In a flash, he took off into the darkness.

8

Sergeant James Gleason's face was beet red. He had just spent five minutes out on the patio calling Pendleton every negative name that popped into his mind. This wasn't like the escape of a hardened criminal in a complicated plot. A simple distraction and a young woman supposedly in police custody was now gone.

"You must find her. You must," Mrs. Menjou moaned, elbows propped on her knees, her face buried in her hands. She sobbed softly as various policemen came in and out reporting to Gleason. He decided that at this point, it would be better to leave the grieving woman alone. Gleason straightened the brim of his hat and prepared to leave when a man showed up at the doorway.

"Who are you?" Gleason demanded.

"Alan Mowbray," the man replied in an offended yet stately British accent, "I'm the Menjou's butler."

"Yeah?" Gleason's eyebrows raised, "and where have you been?"

"I was away for the day but just heard the news and felt it my place to be here with the Mrs."

"Hmmm. Okay. Go ahead. But stay available. We'll want to question you later."

"At your service, sir." Mowbray bowed slightly, passed by Gleason and went to Mrs. Menjou, where he offered condolences and asked for any instructions on what was to be done.

She spoke quietly to him for a moment and then went to the door to see Sergeant Gleason out. "Thank you for your help, Sergeant, but just please, please find that girl."

"Don't you worry, ma'am. We're on it. We'll have her in a jiffy." He snapped his fingers for emphasis. "I'll be in touch with you soon." He pulled the door closed behind him and left.

An eerie calm enveloped the house. Mrs. Menjou stood staring out the window as the police car drove off. The only sound was the careful movement of a butler performing his customary tasks. After the police cars were safely out of sight, Mowbray appeared at the woman's side.

"This Krell girl….," he started.

"Yes, I know," she interrupted.

"I don't like it. I just don't like it at all."

"Mowbray, it had to be done. I had no choice."

"I know, but I have a feeling this is not going to turn out well."

"It already hasn't," she said, slowly and sadly heading off to her empty bedroom.

9

Eve was crouched behind a row of tall filing cabinets. She peeked into the overly bright office area to see if it was clear to go the four feet to her right to reach the steps to the dungeon. It was empty except for two men chatting at the desk near the front door.

She recognized Lionel Atwill, the funeral director, in his standard jet black overcoat, pin-striped suit and top hat. She could not see the other man's face, but from the emphatic tone of his voice and the large bulky silhouette of his frame it was obviously Walter Slezak, the owner of the butcher shop on Witherspoon Street. They were both probably there to leave their submissions for the paper: death notices for one, this week's price of ground beef for the other. They were heavily engaged in conversation, seemingly oblivious to the loud battle going on between Mr. Mitchell and Spring Byington.

"What's the matter with him?" Mitchell was yelling. "All I wanted was a simple, plain, easy, short piece on the Princeton-Yale game."

"I know, Mr. Mitchell, but…."

"Do I get that? Noooooo."

"He's upset. His girlfriend has…." Spring tried to give an excuse for Gordon.

"This was BEFORE all this happened, Miss Byington. Before. This assignment should have been HERE," the sound of his hand pounding his desk reverberated throughout the room, "on my desk BEFORE any of this happened. No. Look what he gave me. One page on the game and one page on this Bund thing. I did not ask for a story about some immigrant group holding get-togethers or picnics or whatever. And then look… look, Miss Byington. A page about what? What is this? A page about a word in the dictionary. 'Dord.' What is that? Who cares? Who would want to read that? I mean, are we doing vocabulary lessons in The Topic now?"

"But sir," Eve could hear Spring trying to calm her boss.

"To top it all off," Mitchell was in full fury, "look here. One page of each. He didn't even leave me the complete piece on even one of these stories! Poor excuse for journalism…."

Eve was frozen behind the filing cabinets, wanting to jump out and defend Gordon. But when she looked up and saw the two men still engrossed in their chat, she realized that she had to get to the cellar stairway. Taking a deep breath, she tip-toed quickly to the steps. As she descended into the dungeon, she could hear Mitchell yelling, "He's fired! This time, he's really and truly fired!"

10

A dimly lit stairway led to a crowded cellar filled mostly by a massive printing press in the center of the cramped space. Work tables covered with papers and printing equipment filled the balance of the room.

"Anybody home?" Eve softly asked. A face popped up from behind the printing press, very nearly sending Eve to an early grave.

"Hello." It was the soft-spoken voice of a balding man with what remained of his hair grouped into scraggly grey outlines over his ears. "Donald. Donald Meek's the name. Guardian of the Dungeon, as they say. And you must be Eve?"

She nodded.

"A pleasure to meet you, I'm sure. I hope you don't mind if I keep working while we talk. I'm just having a bit of a problem with one of the doo-hickeys on the press. Too bad Gordon's not here right now. He could fix it in two shakes of a lamb's tail." Meek noticed Eve's demeanor change from frightened to sad when he mentioned Gordon, so he stopped his work and came out to properly greet her. He was a short man, even shorter than Eve, with droopy overalls and an oversized smock tied around his neck and waist. His looks were generally unimpressive.

"Come on over here, Eve," he said, gently gliding her over to a far corner. "This is Gordon's spot and where he asked me to let you, shall we say, 'hide out' for now." It was a tiny alcove in the darkest area of the cellar. The wall had a three foot section jutting out, possibly intended as a storage area or to coincide with a dump for coal delivery. It had been redecorated, though, and now contained an upholstered chair, frayed at the seams that, as Donald pointed out by pressing his hands down on the cushions, was very, very comfortable. There was also a tiny table with space enough to hold maybe one book and a cup of tea. It sat pressed between the chair and the wall. There was a curtain hanging precariously along a broom handle that had been nailed to the ceiling.

"Not good enough to hide someone from a careful search, but for most of the busy-bodies popping their heads down the stairs to get nosy about what's going on in the dungeon," he put his hands and arms out widely, "it's only me they'll see down here."

Eve smiled, maybe for the first time all day.

"Now, how about a nice cup of tea?" He pulled the curtain aside further to reveal a tea kettle sitting on a hot plate.

"That would be nice," she agreed.

He pulled open a drawer and removed a cigar box, opened it and gingerly removed two sugar cubes. "Two sugars okay?"

"Um, I usually use five."

"Sweet tooth, eh?"

He put the whole open cigar box in front of Eve and placed the cup of hot tea and a spoon beside them. "Gordon said you were a sweet girl," he smiled at her and she looked up, embarrassed. He started back to work, sitting on a bench at a table near Eve, setting blocks of type.

"Now I can tell you're worried and I haven't heard all the details, but from what Gordon's told me, you're a smart girl and he's pretty bright himself, so if anybody can get out of a mess like this, you two can."

"I just don't know how, Mr. Meek," Eve replied.

"Now, now, Eve," he tried again to calm her, "you know Gordon – how he can see the future. Not like some silly made-up psychic thing-a-ma-bob, but more like, well, I think maybe it's from him reading H.G. Wells, Jules

Verne, all those things. He doesn't get visions or use supernatural hocus pocus. He figures out the future. He sees things and puts them together and figures out what happens next. You know, I'm going to tell you my favorite prediction of his, which he tells me at least once a week. Gordon says that about six months ago, he was at a dance on a Saturday night. It was really crowded, you couldn't even move. There were so many people, friends from school, strangers, faces he recognized from seeing them pass by in the street. But, then, and when he tells me this he always slows the words to close to a halt - for emphasis – all the way over on the other side of the hall he could see a cute girl with big brown eyes and dark curly hair. And then, Gordon always stops completely and looks at me, then he says 'It's the best proof that I can see the future, Donald. You see, I knew right at that moment I was going to marry that girl.'"

11

Eve burst into tears. Meek, feeling horrible that he had brought this on, tried to console her. "I am so sorry. I didn't mean to…."

Sobbing, she broke in, "No. No. It wasn't your fault. I just started to think. Now there's no way we could ever be married. Never. It's hopeless."

"No, no, dear. It will work out, you'll see."

"No. Don't you see. I'm wanted for murder. I'm a fugitive, accused by one of the bastions of the community. And even if by some miracle I managed to clear myself, I just overheard Mr. Mitchell say he's firing Gordon. My father already doesn't like Gordon and would never, ever consent to us getting married now. Father is always complaining about him for one reason or another, and what would he think, Gordon being fired from the newspaper." She buried her head in her hands, and silently wept.

"Eve… Mitchell fires everyone at The Topic at least once a day."

"But, he sounded so angry."

"Well, maybe he fires Gordon a little more than the rest of us, but don't worry."

A new thought came to him and he went over to the printing press, fooled with a handle, pulled down a lever and then carefully balanced a football on top of it. He moved a couple of chairs out of the way so that it was clear from the press all the way to one wall. He removed a leather football helmet from a peg on the coat rack. As he carefully pulled it over his head, he began explaining to Eve, "Gordon's not going to be stuck at this newspaper forever. You know how handy he is – fixing just about anything. Now, I've worked on old Bessie here," he tapped lovingly on the printing press, "for over 20 years. I know it inside and out. Yet when something breaks down, as happens often with a veteran like this, I can be fiddling around for hours – my ears turning red trying to figure out how to fix it – and in walks Gordon. He stares at it for a few minutes, his hands folded across his chest. You can see the gears spinning around in his mind and then zip-zap! It's up and running like new."

"Now," he continued, "you combine that with his ability to figure out the future, and you have something new. He keeps calling it multi-use or something, but it's going to lead to something big."

"Uh, what does this have to do with football?" Eve was more than puzzled.

"Heh-heh," Meek pooh-poohed her question. "That's

what I was just getting to. Now, this is not some world-changing invention but a, shall we say, a shape of things to come. Gordon knows that I'm stuck down in this dark dungeon, no windows, no contact with the outside world for most of the day. So, nice chap that he is, he invented a diversion for me. Now, just watch."

He took a firm stance two feet from the printing press, threw a switch and looked up. As the press locked gears and started to turn, the lever jerked forward and flipped the football across the room. It was a perfect spiral, too, as if the best quarterback in the Ivy League had just thrown it. Meek rushed from his starting position across the room and caught the ball smoothly with both hands. Turning his head slightly toward Eve for acknowledgment, he jutted his arm out into his best Knute Rockne imitation and dodged imaginary tacklers, even assisted one of them by falling down, purposely, just short of the wall. "Down on the three yard line!" he proclaimed, flashing a huge grin from the floor.

Eve's lips curled into a soft smile, "Now, you'll have to admit that a football-throwing printing press is not exactly the next electric light bulb." Meek nodded in agreement. "But," she continued, sometimes one thing leads to another, and I have to agree, this could just be one of many great things to come. By the way… you're on the two yard line, not the three yard line."

"This is the three yard line," he responded emphatically.

"Two," she retorted.

"Three. It's always been the three yard line."

"Measure it then, Mr. Meek. Don't you have a ruler or a yard stick?"

He hopped up, went behind the press and brought back a long wooden yard stick, which he defiantly put down against the wall. When he lined it up against the football, it was exactly two yards. "To the inch! You're right. Amazing!"

"Thank you very much."

"How did you do that?" he asked.

"You know my father, Karl, right? His used furniture store? Well, he's always measuring something – a dresser, a bed, a dining room table, the space to put the table, a couch. And ever since I was old enough to walk, I followed him around all day. He'd call me his pretty little shadow. If he was going up to New Brunswick or Jersey City to buy a lot of desks, I'd be right there while he was measuring each one. Trying to fit a king-size bed through an apartment entrance, over a banister and up a narrow winding staircase and into a one-room flat, I'd be there while he was measuring. My father started to make it into a game. After he taught me yards, feet, inches, quarter inches, I would have to guess each measurement. 'Okay,' he'd say, pointing his yardstick toward a writing desk, 'how wide?' I would get treats sometime and always big hugs, and now I can spot a quarter inch at 300 feet."

"Seriously?" Meek replied in awe.

"Well, that is a bit of an exaggeration, but it's become as matter of fact as reading. My father does say that it can be…. Oh my gosh! I just thought of it. My parents. They don't even know about any of this."

"Eve, I don't think it would be wise for you to try to get in touch with them. The police might be watching. Would you like me to try and get a message to them?" Meek offered.

"Oh, you know, they might not even be home yet. They drove down to Atlantic City for the week-end, so they probably won't be back until tomorrow morning. Maybe if we can figure out how to contact them in the morning?"

"Don't you worry, Eve," he reassured her, "we'll get through to them. Maybe they can help. Hey, maybe Gordon can help us get a message to them."

Instead of being hopeful, Eve became increasingly worried. "Where is he, by the way? He said he would be right back. It's been too long. I hope he's all right."

12

Detective Sergeant James Gleason put his well-worn shoes up on his desk. His wide brimmed cap was perched back a little on his thin bald head. The door was closed and his office was quiet. This case just needed a little thinking, and he was now in his favorite spot for doing just that.

What could have been Eve's motive, he wondered. It just didn't make sense. She was a smart girl from a good family, a regular boyfriend working for the newspaper, no previous problems. What could....

Pendleton burst into the office, his hat in his hand. "Chief, I just thought of something. Radits, that guy from the paper, I betcha he's the one that kidnapped the girl."

Gleason started to cut in, but Pendleton kept on, his hands outstretched to cut off an interruption from his boss. "Now, you gotta listen, Chief. I was just thinking. Radits was in the room with us when Mrs. Menjou accused that dame of the murder. But," and he paused and assumed a sense of pride in his deductive talents, "but the next thing you know, he's gone. He must've slipped out and set up that distraction to steal the car and the girl." Pendleton was beaming as he finished.

Gleason, on the other hand, looked like he was ready to burst. "Pendleton," he started slowly, "the Mrs. and I, we go to the pictures every once in awhile. And she likes those detective pictures, you know. But every time we get out of the theater, she always says to me, 'Jimmy,' she calls me Jimmy. 'Jimmy,' she says to me, 'how come they always make the police so stupid in these pictures? They are just so dumb. How come they do that?' And you know what I tell her?" he paused for an answer, but Pendleton just looked puzzled. "I say: real life, dear. Real life."

Gleason's tone quickly switched from reflective to angry. "Of course it was Radits, you lame-brained moron. Who else do you think we put an all points bulletin out on… Mickey Mouse? Listen, I've got O'Malley watching the apartment house down at 26 Witherspoon. I want you to go down and relieve O'Malley. Keep an eye out for Eve or her parents coming home. We still haven't been able to contact them. And Radits, too. Got it? Any of them. Anything suspicious. Now get going before I demote you to street sweeper! And stop calling me Chief!"

"Sure, Chief. Okay, Chief," Pendleton mumbled, backing out of the office.

Gleason rolled his eyes and let them wander around the room. Maybe it's time to retire, he thought. His eyes settled on a picture of himself from 1914, when he was the lightweight champion boxer of Jersey City - arms posed as if giving a left jab. He cherished those memories. The gimp leg he suffered in the Great War ended those dreams, but he still loved the fight. More than this, he thought, thinking again of Pendleton. "I know," he thought, "maybe I'll retire and find a promising young boxer to manage. That's something I could enjoy." He tipped the brim of his hat over his eyes, put his feet back up on the desk and nodded off to sleep.

13

Gordon was crouched down behind some trash cans in the narrow alley across from the front of 26 Witherspoon Street. Slezak's Butcher Shop and Urkin's Hardware book-ended the alley. The two day old meat scraps that filled one of the metal garbage cans were giving off such a putrid odor that Gordon held pages from a discarded magazine in front of his nose, hoping to block at least some of the offensive aromas. He was also getting frustrated that Officer O'Malley was still sitting in his car directly in front of number 26, staked out for him or Eve.

When Mrs. Menjou had raised her hand to point the finger of blame at Eve, something clicked in his head – like a camera had snapped a picture. He immediately placed her, earlier in the day, in the exact same dress and hat, inside 26 Witherspoon Street. It had been very early in the morning, he thought maybe around eight o'clock, and he was supposed to be on his way to interview the Princeton football coach about the upcoming game against Yale. Gordon thought he would just make a quick stop to see Eve, maybe have a cup of coffee and then start his day.

26 Witherspoon had a huge storefront for the "Princeton New and Used Furniture Company" run by Eve's dad, Karl Krell. At the right end of the storefront was a doorway to a steep set of stairs leading to the second floor. The second, third and fourth floors were all laid out as one or two bedroom apartments. On the fifth floor, there was a one room storage area – the attic, really – that had been converted into a rented room for John "Bucky" Carradine, the town drunk.

Bucky had joined the Army in 1918, shortly after his father had been killed in battle in France. Bucky himself had ended up in France in the Meuse-Argonne offensive, where an explosion not ten feet from his trench line had thrown him in the air, knocking him unconscious. He had come to some days later with the dead bodies of his fellow soldiers covered with huge black rats. Bucky had lain there in pain with two broken legs for six more days, inhaling traces of mustard gas from a nearby battle. The crying that started when some British troops found and rescued him did not stop until he took his first swig of straight Scotch. He was still a good person, though, and the kindness shown to him by Eve and the people like her made him more caring and less bitter than others with his experience.

The other odd thing that Gordon remembered was that when he pushed open the heavy front door at the entrance to 26 Witherspoon, there, in the early morning shadows half-way up the steps, was Bucky Carradine and Mrs. Menjou. They were absorbed in a deep, serious conversation. Gordon's appearance in the doorway clearly startled them and they awkwardly switched to meaningless pleasantries as Bucky headed up the stairs, while Mrs. Menjou came down. She exchanged obligatory greetings with Gordon as she passed him, and left the building.

At the time, Gordon had thought nothing more of it. He continued up the steps and knocked on the door of apartment 2A, the residence of the Krell family. After a couple of minutes with no response, he assumed no one was home and headed for his interview. It was only in the light of the events of the afternoon that Gordon replayed that chance meeting. It might have been nothing at all, but now there had been a murder and his girlfriend's life was in jeopardy. Gordon knew about the less than stellar reputation of the police department from his job at The

Topic. It was a small paper in a small town and he'd heard enough from Franchot Tone and others around the paper to realize that he had only one option. He would have to be the one to find the real killer.

He wanted to speak with Mrs. Menjou, confront her with the facts that would disprove her story. But he knew that right now that was impossible. She was most likely locked into the story she told, in addition to being distraught over her husband's death. He would have to bide his time on that front. For now, he would have to look into every other angle. The first was Bucky Carradine.

14

Gordon's hopes that O'Malley might just leave were quickly dashed when Pendleton showed up to relieve him. Gordon's only chance was to try to enter through the rear of the building, and that would be a real task.

He circled all the way around Spring Street, crossed Bridge Street and came back up through Palmer Square. The Square was well lit, but as he turned down Bailey Lane, he entered another small alley that ran along the back of Witherspoon Street. He flattened himself against the concrete wall of the back of number 26. A back door opened down near number 14 or 16 and someone tossed out empty boxes and then slammed the door shut. Again it was dark. He found a sturdy wooden crate, carefully and quietly upended it and placed it close to the bottom rail of the fire escape, grabed onto the rail and pulled himself up. When he reached the second floor hall window, he pried it open and entered onto the staircase landing between the second and third floors. Heading up the stairs, the third and fourth floors were both dimly lit, the only illumination seeped into the hallway from under the doorways of the various apartments on each floor. Just as his foot touched the first step toward the fifth floor, a door opened. Apartment 4C, Gordon realized. A short couple dressed in big heavy overcoats emerged from the flat. The man was carrying three or four packages, all of which appeared to be tied with twine. The woman simply had a pocketbook dangling from her wrist. They tiredly plodded down the stairs, not even noticing Gordon watching them from the shadows in the fifth floor stairwell.

"I've never seen them before," he thought. "Must've just moved in." He returned to his task, quickly reaching the small attic-style space on the fifth floor. Various supplies for the maintenance of the building crowded the small area outside Bucky's door. It was just about pitch black as he reached the door, no light visible from under the door. He tightly held his breath and knocked.

Gordon waited. There was no response, no sound of movement from within. He tried again, this time a bit louder and for a bit longer. He could hear things falling, as if someone was bumping into things. The door opened and there was Bucky – along with the unmistakable aroma of Scotch.

15

A small nightlight sitting on a bed table gave an eerie glow to the sunken eyes on the face of Bucky Carradine. "Gordon?" Bucky asked in a slow thick voice close to a whisper, "can I help you?"

Gordon pushed past him into the room. "I need to

talk to you for a minute. I'm sorry if I'm disturbing you."

"No, no. Well, uh, it's no trouble at all?" Bucky always seemed unsure, almost a question in every sentence.

"It's about Mrs. Menjou. Can you tell me anything about your chat with her?"

Bucky straightened up a bit, his tall frame towering over Gordon. "Mrs. Menjou, you say? I really don't know her very well. Haven't seen her in quite awhile. Maybe at the market a few weeks ago? Um, no. Sorry. Can't really help you much there. I can't even remember what…."

Gordon broke in. "I saw you talking with her early this morning, Bucky." He pointed toward the doorway. "Downstairs. On the steps."

"Oh. Oh. That slipped my mind," Bucky dismissed it with a wave of his hand. "Just passing pleasantries, you know? Nice weather we're having, Mrs. Menjou."

Gordon could barely contain his frustration. "Look Bucky, you both seemed in a very intense discussion when I walked in the door and it didn't in any way seem like passing pleasantries."

"Well," Bucky replied, "I can only tell you what happened and what happened was nothing happened."

Gordon stared at Bucky's glassy expression. This was obviously not working. "Look," he said, walking around the room as he continued, "I don't know if you heard, but Professor Menjou has been murdered." Bucky gasped at the news. Gordon continued to scan the room, noting how neat and uncluttered it was, except for an overturned milk bottle near the bed and a revolver clumsily hidden and partially protruding from under the mattress. Gordon continued, "What makes this worse is that Mrs. Menjou has accused Eve of the murder." He turned quickly to see Bucky's reaction.

Bucky, with a detached stoicism perhaps aided by the

Scotch, whispered so slowly that the letters in his words seemed to have extra space between them, "I really wish I could help you, Gordon, but I just can't."

Realizing he was at a dead end, Gordon headed for the door. He turned back as he left, "Please, Bucky. If you think of anything that might help, get in touch with me. Eve's life might depend on it." Bucky nodded to him and closed the door.

"What's next," Gordon thought. He was sure that he wasn't through with Bucky. Bucky was obviously lying about the conversation. He had a gun in his room – for what purpose? And why would the town drunk have just about the neatest, well-kept apartment in New Jersey, well, other than the Krell's, that is. Eve's mom kept their place like a showroom. "Oh my gosh!" Gordon blurted out loud in the fourth floor stairway. Eve's parents probably don't know what's going on, he thought, and the police have probably scared them to death, searching their apartment for her. He decided to try to contact them since he was in the building. He quietly made it to the second floor and tapped lightly on the door.

No answer.

He tried a couple more times and then realized that with the police stationed at the front door, he shouldn't take any more chances in that building. He headed back toward the window he had used to enter the building, looking both ways as he moved from shadow to shadow in the hallway. He stopped in his tracks, holding his breath when he noticed two eyes peering through a cracked open door at apartment 2B. He realized it was just nosy Edna May Oliver, an old spinster woman who lived alone. Her long narrow face was made for looking through cracks in doors, watching who went where with whom at any time of the day or night. He waited patiently until she retracted her face back inside her apartment and closed the door. He dashed over to the window and had one leg over the sill when he thought for sure he'd heard a footstep behind him clicking on the linoleum floor. He started to turn his head when a loud scream came from Miss Oliver's room – just as something hit him on the head and everything went black.

16

Gordon woke up on a coarse hard couch in Miss Oliver's apartment. His head was pounding and Miss Oliver's stern face was just inches from his as she pressed a wet, cold towel to his temple.

"That's some wallop you took, Mr. Radits."

"Well, I…," he tried to speak, but she quickly shushed him.

"No, don't you talk right now, young man. You need to get your senses about you. Now what were you doing trying to climb out of a window at this time of night?" A thought came to her and she modified her question. "Actually, there is NO time of the day or night that you should be climbing out of windows, especially in buildings in which you do not live. Now tell me. What were you doing?"

"Well," he started, but again Miss Oliver interrupted. "Perhaps I should call the police?" She waited to see his reaction.

Gordon sat straight up, knocking the towel out of her hand, his head throbbing like crazy. "No, please don't call…."

She pushed him back down onto the couch, the back

of his head landing a little too harshly on the armrest.

"Sorry," she apologized. "Anyway, I am not going to call the police. What kind of a ninny do you think I am? You and your girlfriend both wanted by the police and I'm going to call them to report your climbing out a second story window in the dark? Now you just lay there until you've got your wits about you again, if you ever did have any, and then we'll see what's to be done." She pushed her chair back and got up. "I'll go make you a nice cup of hot tea. You just stay cozy right there." She marched off across the room.

How did Miss Oliver know about Eve? What am I thinking, Gordon caught himself, this lady knows everything that goes on in Princeton!

"I thought I heard someone knocking on my door," Miss Oliver said, setting a delicate gold rimmed tea cup on the table next to Gordon. That was her stock answer for why she was always peeping out of her doorway. "Just as I opened it, I saw a figure in the shadows right behind you. It had some big thing in its hand – a club or something. I could see the man's arm raised to hit you over the head. I screamed. It must have scared the attacker enough that he only hit you a glancing blow."

"Feels like a lot more than GLANCING," Gordon moaned.

"Well, if that's not gratitude," she smiled. "See if I scream next time you're being attacked. Now, I know all about the murder charge against Eve, but what did you hope to accomplish sneaking into her apartment tonight – some evidence or something?"

Gordon couldn't tell whether Edna May was trying to help with really solving this dilemma or if she was just snooping for more gossip. He decided to trust her.

"I wasn't here to get in Eve's apartment. I was here to

see Bucky."

"Hmmm." She pressed her lips together into one straight line. "And what would John Carradine have to do with this murder?"

"I really don't know if there's a connection, but I had to start somewhere. Mrs. Menjou is accusing Eve of the murder, so I'm starting with her. I saw her early this morning talking with Bucky right in the stairway outside, sort of an odd couple, I thought, and it seemed like a serious conversation. But, according to Bucky, it wasn't."

"It was."

"No. Bucky said it wasn't."

"No," Miss Oliver retorted, "I say it was. You see, I thought I heard the milkman at the door this morning and when I opened the door, what did I see but John Carradine and Abigail Menjou engaged in a very intense and confusing conversation. They were talking very quietly when I first opened the door but as the conversation became more heated, their voices rose. Actually, it was John that kept trying to calm Abigail down. He kept saying, 'It will work' or 'It will work out,' something like that. And, oh yes, a number of times she repeated either, 'They know' or 'He knows,' I'm not sure which one. But John's big back was to me and though I'm not certain, it appeared to me that she opened her pocketbook and took out a small package and handed it to John. I think she was ready to say something else to him but the front door opened and they acted like two deer caught in the headlights. They just stopped dead in their tracks, their conversation ended right there and then, and they went their separate ways."

"That was me at the door," Gordon interjected.

"Well, I'm sorry. I didn't know that. As soon as John headed up the stairs, I closed my door."

"That sheds some light on that meeting. They did look like a strange pair to be sharing such a private discussion. It seems that they had something they were trying to hide." Gordon was thinking out loud, "Do you think Bucky could have been the one to shoot the Professor?"

"Oh my goodness," Edna May sat straight up. "I don't believe he could do that."

"Well, do you think he could've been the one that clunked me over the head?"

She waved her hands to dismiss the notion. "Absolutely not." The doubt on her face did not match the certainty of her words.

"Well, then. Who did?"

This was Miss Oliver's chance and she jumped right in. "Now, I try to mind my own business around here, but they've been letting a lot of riff-raff move in here lately. And I wouldn't put it past any of them. Take the Kibbees, for example, up on the fourth floor. Mrs. Kibbee is very nice. Ailene's her name. Works her fingers to the bone keeping food on the table. Not only does she keep her home spotless, she takes in laundry to pay the bills. Why, she must keep half the population of Princeton in clean clothes. And their daughter, Shirley, sweet as a button – adopted, you know – but I don't hold that against her. Just the strangest thing: she calls her father "Captain." Not Daddy. Not Pop. Just "Captain." And that's the one thing he's not. If I've ever seen such a good-for-nothing, well, I just don't know. He must roll out of bed by sunrise just to get out of the house so he doesn't have to help out. Every morning, seven days a week, tip-toeing down the stairs like he's off to work. But does he ever work? No siree. He's tried out every park bench in town by the end of the day. You might recognize him, because I'm sure you've seen him. Always has a bag of peanuts to feed the squirrels – and himself – and a newspaper."

She spared no wrath for poor Mr. Kibbee. "That paper looks so worn out the end of the day, he must have read it through 20 times. And I know one thing, there's not a job anywhere where they'll pay you to feed the squirrels and read the newspaper."

Edna May left the Kibbees and moved on to the next apartment. "Here's a strange one - Mr. Roland Young in 3B. Now, why would a banker move out of a nice home in Lawrenceville with a bit of land and take a small flat downtown? Now some people say it's just to be close to work, just up the corner at the First National Bank and Trust, and I have to admit he seems to work quite a bit, but I think it's something else. Do you know the man talks to himself? And the walls? Don't shake your head – I've seen it with my own two eyes. Walking not ten feet behind him along Nassau Street when all of a sudden he stops dead in his tracks, brushes his shoulder as if something is on it and then shakes his fist at the air or the wall of the building or who knows what. A man like that, he's loopy. Who knows what he's capable of?"

3C was next on the list. "Then, there's…" she stopped. "Wait. Shhh." She put up her hand for Gordon to be quiet, even though she hadn't let him get a word in edgewise for a full five minutes. Apparently Edna May could hear something, and Miss Oliver had hearing that could detect a good night kiss at three hundred paces through a set of doors and down two flights of stairs. "There's someone at the door," she whispered.

Suddenly there was a loud pounding on the door. Gordon quickly looked around the room. Edna May pointed toward a closet. Gordon quietly rushed over and crouched down behind the coats. If it was the police, he thought, my goose is cooked.

17

The pounding on the door was repeated. Edna May made sure that Gordon was shut in the closet and then opened her front door. It was Bucky.

"Sorry, Miss Oliver. I'm out of Scotch. I was wondering if…."

"My word!" she cut in, fuming. "You're interrupting my sleep at this time of night to borrow alcoholic beverages?"

"But Miss O…"

"Now you forget about it and go right upstairs and sleep it off. Good night!" She slammed the door in his face.

She waited, her face pressed against the door until she heard Bucky's footsteps disappear up the steps. Then she called Gordon out of the closet. This time he decided to sit up at the kitchen table, since he had been getting quite sleepy on the couch. When Edna May told him that it was Bucky asking for Scotch, something about the incident jumped out at him, but before he could say anything, she was back to her list of suspects as if she had never been interrupted. "In 3C, that's Mr. Allen Jenkins. Now there's a man who never pays his rent, from what I hear. He's a real animal lover – horses, in particular. Just about every time we meet, I'll start a conversation and maybe I'll say 'What a sunny day, Mr. Jenkins' and he'll say 'Sunny Day – yes, that's it, Miss Oliver. Sunny Day's a horse I'm kinda fond of' and he'll mumble some nonsense about luck and off he goes. What an unusual quirky behavior."

"But," she continued, "if you think that's quirky, try the next flat for slimy behavior. Just moved in last week, a Mr. Roscoe Karns. Some sort of salesman. Or, should I say, every sort of salesman. He's introduced himself to me three times in the week he's lived here and already tried to sell me life insurance, pots and pans, and an elixir that cures liver spots. Why, every single meeting we've had he's shaken my hand and I immediately checked my handbag to make sure nothing was missing. But, he really does have a pleasant smile." She finished with a slight grin, and then moved on.

"Now, I could go on like this all day. Every one of these people could be totally innocent or they could have some reason to do you harm. But right now we need to get our priorities straight."

"Okay," Gordon nodded, not knowing where this was heading.

"Where's Eve?" She certainly got straight to the point.

18

"I don't know where..." he started, not sure exactly how much to say.

"Don't you lie to me, Gordon Radits." Edna May stuck her pointed finger right up to his nose. "Now, you know I'm on your side. I'm going to help you and Eve get out of this mess." She paused and her face softened, "You don't think I'd give away a young couple in love, do you?"

Gordon couldn't argue with that logic. He knew they needed people like Edna May on their side. She knew so much about everyone in town, whether it was all true or not was another story. "She's safe in the cellar of The Topic office."

"We need to get you over to her," Edna May said. "With that bump on your head, I'm sure you'd rather have her as your nurse than me."

"You've been a perfect nurse, and I appreciate all you've done, Miss Oliver." Gordon stopped as the phone rang.

Edna May went over and answered. The voice on the other end was muffled. "Please give Gordon Radits a message…."

"I don't know who…." Edna May cut in, trying to deny that Gordon was there, but she was immediately interrupted.

"I know he's in your apartment. All I ask is that you forward a message. I have information about the murder of Adolph Menjou. Tell him to meet me in the alley directly behind the shoe store at 18 Witherspoon. I will be there in exactly five minutes. If he is not there, I will leave. Tell him to tell no one or bring no one other than himself." And then there was a click and the voice was gone.

Edna May relayed the message, but warned Gordon not to go. "You're in no condition to go anywhere. Just wait," she pleaded, "there's sure to be another chance."

"No." Gordon stood up and headed for the door. "If I can get any information that might lead to the real killer, I have to take it." Edna May walked with him to the door and watched until he had climbed through the window to head down the fire escape into the alley. The iron grating made a slight clanging noise as he climbed onto it, so he moved cautiously down the rest of the steps.

It was pitch black in the alley. It was nearing midnight and there was not a person to be seen or heard anywhere.

Gordon felt his way along the cement wall, moving toward where he thought the rear of the shoe store would be. Something glistened briefly in front of him and as he took his next step, he tripped over something on the ground. He felt himself falling, the skin on the palms of his outstretched hands scraping hard as they made contact with the sidewalk. He landed on the object and instantly rolled off when he realized it was a person. No, not a person. A body. A body so still that he knew it was dead. As he felt around in the dark, the knife protruding from the body's back instantly confirmed his suspicions.

The sound of Gordon's falling must have generated enough noise to reach the ears of Edna May Oliver, for just at that moment, a light appeared in her kitchen window and her curtains were gently and slowly pulled to the side. That tiny glow allowed Gordon to see that it was a heavyset man with short cropped blond hair laying dead next to him.

Not far down the alley, still completely covered in the darkness, a man was watching the scene. He was pressed against the wall, trying to be silent but close to bursting. His heart raced, his veins bulged and his hands shook uncontrollably. One single silent step at a time he slowly backed up, put up his collar and disappeared down a side street.

19

Was this the person I was supposed to meet? If so, who knew about the meeting and killed him first? Gordon had to think quickly. This person's killer could still be nearby and Gordon had already been clunked once today and that was quite enough. He quickly went through the pockets of the dead man searching for clues. Any clue, any piece of evidence that might help.

A gun.

A piece of paper he couldn't read in the dark.

No identification, wallet or anything else.

Gordon put the piece of paper in his pocket. He couldn't head back into the building, so he got up and walked as fast as he could in the darkness to the end of the alley and turned onto the exact same side street down which another man had just disappeared.

20

Abigail Menjou paced up and down slowly in front of her bed. She thought she had used up every last tear she had, but they just kept coming. Everywhere she looked there was a reminder of Adolph. The bed, the chair in the corner, the robe draped over a hanger. She had taken the two pills prescribed by their longtime friend, Dr. Lew Ayres. They were supposed to calm her nerves and let her get some sleep, but, she contemplated, it might take the whole bottle to do any good.

Her personal history played over and over in her mind. Meeting Adolph in Riga, Latvia. Their whirlwind courtship and the long boat ride to America. The accolades he had received for his abilities as a pianist. His decision for them to settle down in Princeton and to give up performing for teaching had left her with a bitterness that gradually grew to animosity between them. It was only the events of the last four months that had made them put all that aside, and regain what they thought had been lost.

She heard a door being quietly closed.

"Alan? Is that you?" she called.

There was no reply.

She went into the hallway and repeated loudly, "Alan? Is that you?"

Alan Mowbray's head peeked around the corner at the bottom of the staircase.

"Yes, it is. My apologies for disturbing you. I was trying to be as quiet as possible."

"Had you been out?" she inquired.

"Why, yes. I…."

"Was it about half an hour ago that you went out?"

"That's about right…."

"There was a phone call. I heard the phone ring. I'm sure of it. I had been laying down. I got up when I heard the phone ring and yelled down to ask who it was, but all I heard was the door closing. Was that when you went out?"

"Yes. It was about thirty minutes ago when I left."

"Who was on the phone? Was it for me?"

"No. It was a wrong number."

"Oh. Why would we get a wrong number?"

"Now, don't worry. It was nothing. You get some rest like Dr. Ayres ordered. I'll take care of everything."

She vaguely agreed and went back to her pacing.

Mowbray returned to the kitchen where he sat down and removed his shoes. They had blood all over them. He checked up and down and found traces on his pants, too. He would have to change. He would have to dispose of both the shoes and the pants before doing any other thing. He did so with a determined formality. Abigail Menjou must not learn anything about the latest events, he thought. Nor must anyone else.

21

As tired as he was, as wobbly as he still felt from the blow on the head, Gordon still took a long elaborate route to get to The Topic building. One day, he thought, radar will be so advanced that I'd be able to map out my complete route on some sort of device and not have to wander up and down streets – just follow the directions on the map machine. Maybe I'll invent it, he thought. I'll call it the GDS, Gordon's Directions System. The exuberance of that thought quickly dissolved as he realized that if radar became that advanced, then it would probably be able to track him personally. The police would have caught him hours ago, known where Eve was and arrested her right from the get go.

"Oh well," he mumbled. "The future ain't always what you thought it was."

He paused behind some parked cars across from The Topic. The building was completely dark - one of the few times, night or day, when there was no activity. It would soon be the three a.m. starting time for Donald Meek to fire up the presses for the morning edition. Gordon carefully made his way around to the back entrance and slipped into the building. There was one small flickering light in the basement. Donald was flat on his back, laying on a mound of newspaper pages on the floor. Eve was fast asleep, curled up on the big chair in the hidden corner of the room.

Gordon wanted so badly to rush over and reassure her that everything would be okay, but he knew the sleep would do them both good. He found a spot on the floor, near Eve's corner. He grabbed some rags from a table, piled them up behind his head as a pillow and effortlessly fell off to sleep.

22

Detective Sergeant James Gleason carefully maneuvered into his office, a stack of papers in one hand and a steaming mug of coffee in the other. He used the back of his shoe to kick the door closed behind him. To his surprise the coroner, Eric Blore, was already occupying his seat. "What's the meaning of this, Blore?" he snapped.

"Well, good morning to you, too, Sergeant," Blore replied.

"Yeah, good morning," Gleason reluctantly mumbled. "I didn't think there were enough dead bodies to get you up this early, Blore, and," he added, "get outta my chair!"

"Well, didn't someone wake up on the wrong side of the police car," Blore said as he rose from the chair, revealing a long tan overcoat and a bright red bow-tie.

"Snazzy duds there. I think you'll easily win Coroner Fashion Plate of the Month." Gleason sat down, pretending to readjust the chair as if the coroner had altered it to make it uncomfortable. He dropped the stack of papers on his desk, sending some of them cascading to the floor. Blore reacted quickly and stopped the balance of the pile dead in its tracks.

"Gee, thanks," Gleason said. "Now what d'ya want?"

"I thought you might like some details on the Menjou case, but if you're in no hurry, I can come back next week. Or, how would next spring be?"

"Oh, don't go getting all bent out of shape. I just haven't finished my coffee yet." Gleason showed Blore the half-full cup, the excuse for his sour disposition. "What have you got?"

"Well," Blore started, almost bubbling with the opportunity to relay the results of his expertise, "the bullet was fired from a distance of roughly 10 to 15 feet…"

"Can't you be more exact?" Gleason asked.

"No," Blore blurted out. "The bullet pierced the victim's heart and caused death within sixty seconds. It would appear that the weapon was a Luger."

"Hmmmm." Gleason leaned back in his chair and stared at the ceiling. "This sheds some interesting light on the case. For instance, do we know whether Eve Krell is a shooting expert? I would seriously doubt that."

"My thoughts exactly, Sergeant," Blore chimed in.

"See, I just don't get it. Mrs. Menjou was positive about what happened. There was no doubt at all in her voice. And she and her husband, they were like this," he wrapped two fingers together, "so, she couldn't have had anything to do with it."

"Well, Sergeant, I'd love to help you more, but right now I have a couple more autopsies I'm looking forward to, so I'll have to be leaving."

"Sure. Sure, Blore. Thanks. And if you find any more details, be sure to let me know."

Alone with the report, Gleason felt uneasy with the new information. It never seemed like an open and shut case. Eve never appeared to be even remotely like a murder suspect. But the coroner's report had raised more questions than it answered. Mrs. Menjou had been too upset last night and Gleason wanted to give her a bit of time, but he was itching to go back over and interview her again about the details.

23

Edna May Oliver left her apartment and marched up Witherspoon Street, a picnic basket on her left arm. Covered with a folded red and white checkered tablecloth, the basket was heavy to the point of causing her whole body to tilt as she walked. As she approached the corner of Nassau and Witherspoon, Roland Young was busy with May Robson, the sweet old woman who had a small stand selling shiny red apples.

"But I don't want an apple, I tell you!" Young was protesting as a fine McIntosh appeared to float up into his hand.

"Well then, put it back," May said, grabbing it from the reluctant customer.

"Sorry," he said as he hurried off into the bank building, muttering, "Don't do that again!" to no one in sight.

Apples. That would be a great idea, Edna May thought. She handed Miss Robson some coins and added two apples to her basket. With the load now even heavier, she was huffing and puffing by the time she reached The Topic office. Pausing for a moment to catch her breath, she peered through the storefront glass window. Only Miss Byington was inside, busily typing at a frantic pace. Edna May did not know whether Spring was aware of the hidden occupants in the cellar, so she quickly devised an appropriate strategy.

"Well, good morning, Spring," she sang as she entered the office. "Beautiful fall weather, wouldn't you say?"

"Why, Edna May. It's so nice to see you," Spring stopped typing to greet the visitor. "What can I do for you this morning?"

"Well, I just made this nice basket full of homemade goodies, you know, for Mr. Meek and so I'll just toddle on down and surprise him."

Spring jumped in front of Edna May. "Mr. Meek is frightfully busy at the moment, and, uh, no one is allowed in the dungeon while the press is running. If you would like to leave the basket with me, I'll make sure he gets it." She reached out to grab the picnic basket but Edna May pulled it back away from her.

"I'm sure that's very gracious of you, but Mr. Meek and I have become, how should I put it, very close and these items are very personal in nature." She beamed, very proud of the story she had just concocted.

"My gosh," Spring said, still blocking the way to the steps. "I had no idea about you and Mr. Meek. That is just so nice. But still, I have my orders." She placed herself firmly in the way, determined not to budge. When the telephone rang, she looked at the phone and then at Edna May. Miss Oliver had trouble containing a big grin.

The phone kept ringing.

"Miss Byington! Will you please answer that phone!" a very annoyed Mr. Mitchell yelled from his office.

"Now, don't you move, Edna May. I just have to answer the phone."

"I wouldn't think of such a thing," Edna May replied, her feet ready to propel her forward.

Miss Byington rushed over to the phone and within a split second, Edna May was on her way toward the steps, her hurried stride making her head and neck bob up and down like an ostrich.

"Princeton Topic, may I help you?" Spring moaned into the phone, defeated in a battle of wills due to a silly phone call.

24

As she reached the bottom of the steps, the roaring of the printing press drowned out the sound of Gordon tackling Donald Meek, who was running with a football toward the wall.

"Four and one-half yard line," Eve yelled.

The two men got up off the floor, grabbed a yardstick and measured off the distance. "Amazing," they said in unison, "exactly four and a half yards."

"Uh-hummm," Edna May loudly cleared her throat to get their attention. They turned in surprise, then dashed to greet her as Donald shut down the printing press. Edna May Oliver was not happy.

"Here I am. Worried. Sick out of my mind about the two of you. Not a wink of sleep all night. In the kitchen at sunrise making you fried chicken, my fancy dumplings, a peach cobbler pie. And then, I make a hot pot of tea and stop for a couple of sweet ripe apples. Have they eaten anything, I say to myself? Are they starving? Is poor Gordon's head sore from that thumping? Is Eve worried sick about the police? So I rush over here and what do I find? I find the three of you playing some kind of silly game!"

"It's just Gordon's football-throwing printing press invention, Miss Oliver. We were just…" Eve's explanation was cut off.

"Miss Oliver! You are a life saver. We're famished!" Gordon gave her a big hug as he tried to peek in the picnic basket.

Edna May playfully slapped his hand. "You sit down.

I'll dole it all out while you explain to me what's going on."

She went over to a table and with the back of her hand brushed all the printing supplies over to one side. Donald held his breath at the mess she made. She pulled the checkered tablecloth off of the basket and placed it down on the table, then methodically placed each item on the table.

Spring came rushing down the steps to apologize for not adequately guarding the cellar. After she was filled in, she relaxed and then filled herself up on a great big slice of peach cobbler. When the irritated voice of Mr. Mitchell beckoned her, Spring promised to be a better gate keeper and headed back up to the office.

Eve and Gordon had both slept good but were sore, achy and worried. They ran through all the events of the previous day in detail, over and over, trying to make head or tail out of ever more mysterious events. With both of them being sought after by the police, Edna May suggested that it might be difficult for them to get around. When Gordon pointed out that Officer Pendleton was the most accomplished policeman on the force, they unanimously agreed that unless they physically ran into one of Princeton's finest, they would, in fact, be quite safe.

They had a lot of questions that needed answering. Who was it that called Professor Menjou right before he was killed? What did he mean when he said 'they know about us?' Know what? Gordon decided he would go to the telephone office and try to trace where the call had come from. Eve was concerned about who had hit Gordon over the head and about the murder in the alley, but above all, she couldn't get Mrs. Menjou's accusation out of her mind. Before any of it, though, she wanted to get word to her parents about the situation. "I can't call them. I can't go there," she said to the group. "We know they're watching for me."

"As far as I know," Miss Oliver broke in, "they have not returned home yet. Atlantic City, you said. Hmmm. If they stayed overnight, they might have run into traffic on the way home."

Eve nodded in agreement.

"I'm in the apartment right down the hall," Edna May offered. "If I see them come in, I'll quietly fill them in. I'll make sure they know you're safe."

"Gordon," Spring whispered from the stairs, "I just got the second call from Mr. Slezak in less than an hour. He said that if I saw you to let you know he has some exclusive news for your Princeton-Yale game story this week. He said it's a scoop that won't last long and you better hot-foot it over there as soon as possible."

"If he calls again, just say… I'm on another story, but… I'll be sure to come over when I can." He turned to Eve, "A football story? Not top of the list right now, huh?"

They returned to their plan of action – fine-tuning how they would prove Eve innocent. Edna May offered to return to her home and not only keep an eye out for Mr. and Mrs. Krell, but to keep watch on all the suspicious characters at 26 Witherspoon Street. She began to pack up what was left from the picnic lunch. "My goodness. Only crumbs left. You people eat like pigs!"

"It's your cooking… it's too delicious to leave a single morsel," Gordon answered.

Edna May put the tablecloth back on top of the basket and headed out, giving a little wink to Miss Byington on the way. "We're on the same side," she whispered, then headed out the door and across the street. Just as she turned the corner, she looked back only to see a police car pull up in front. Sergeant Gleason and Officer

Pendleton got out and headed into the building.

25

The wiry detective pushed open the door. His eyes crossed the room slowly from one side to the other. "Good morning, Miss Byington," he said.

She looked up, trying to hide her dismay at his arrival. "A good morning to you, too, Sergeant. How may I help you?"

"Well, we have another murder, Miss Byington. In the alley behind Witherspoon Street."

"Oh my gosh!" she exclaimed. "Who was killed?"

"Well, right now we don't have that information. It was a man in his early 20's, heavyset, short blonde hair, but no identification on him. No wallet, no keys, nothing. The thing is, a couple of people in the area have claimed they saw a figure coming out of the alleyway late last night heading in this general direction."

"Well now, Sergeant," Spring pointed out, "from the alleyway, this direction just means the southern side of Princeton, not the northern side. That's not really much to go on."

"Yes, I know that," Gleason shot back, "but the man's description is fuzzy because it was dark. The consensus seems to be that the silhouette the witnesses saw matches the short stature of Gordon Radits."

"My, that still seems a bit vague, Sergeant."

"Miss Byington," Gleason's rising blood pressure was beginning to show on his face, "it's like this…"

"Like a needle in a haystack, you mean."

"Look, Miss Byington. I need to search the premises

of The Topic building. We have two murders on our hands here. This is serious business and we have Eve Krell and your sports reporter, Gordon Radits, both missing. We've had the Trenton police check his home and there's no sign he's been there in the last forty-eight hours. Neither of them have been to her home, which I might add, we've been keeping under constant surveillance."

"Oh," she interjected, "and isn't that right where you said the second murder took place?"

"It was behind the building and a couple of doors down…."

"Oh. So then the second murder didn't take place right under your nose?" Spring asked in the most sickeningly sweet innocent manner.

"Miss Byington. I am investigating two murders. For the last time, two murders! I am looking for Gordon Radits and I NEED TO SEARCH THIS BUILDING!"

Suddenly a loud voice boomed from Grant Mitchell's office. "GORDON? GORDON RADITS? Did I hear someone say Gordon Radits?" He rushed out of his office. "Gleason, did I hear you say you found that poor excuse for a journalist?"

"No, I…."

"Wait 'til I get my hands on that young good-for-nothing. First, I'll fire him. Then I'll fire him again, if that's possible. And then I just might very well strangle him with my own two hands… where is he??"

"No, no, no, Mitchell. I don't…."

"I have scoured every inch of this building," Mitchell ignored Gleason and kept ranting as he paced past the sergeant and then back to him, "just trying for one minute - one second even – to get a hold of him and let him know how much he's ruined the schedule for printing this newspaper. Why, do you know I had to put in an extra free copy of an advertisement for Lux soap to make up for the copy we were missing because of Radits! Now, where is he? Do you have him down at the jail?"

"You say you've looked over every inch of this building and no sign of him?" Gleason ignored Mitchell's question and asked one himself.

"I just told you that!" Mitchell shouted. "Where is he?"

"Um. We don't have him."

"Don't have him? My god, Gleason. Then what are you doing here?" Mitchell grabbed hold of the sergeant's arm and led him out the door. "Now go find him. And the second you do, you let me know so I can come right down and give him a piece of my mind."

"I'll be sure to do that, Mitchell." Gleason straightened the brim on his hat and headed back to the car. My god, he thought to himself, if Radits ever did show up in the Topic building, they would have to come back and arrest Mitchell for murder.

26

Spring Byington was standing behind her desk, her mouth wide open, speechless. She did not know what to think. Gleason had just come within a hair's breadth of finding Eve and Gordon for sure and only the ranting of Mitchell had dissuaded him from his search. But, she thought, Mr. Mitchell's blood pressure must be through the roof. This time for sure he would really fire Gordon.

"I'll get you one of your pills, sir," Spring volunteered, pouring a cup of water from the cooler and heading to the cabinet.

"You can skip that, Miss Byington. I'm fine."

"But, Mr. Mitchell, you know what happens when you get so excited. The doctor said to take your pill as soon as possible."

"I am not excited," he replied. He started to walk past her to head to the steps to the cellar. She jumped in front of him, fearing he might actually go down to the cellar and who knew how that would end.

"I really think you don't look good, sir. Your face is all flushed. I just feel it would be better for you to sit down for a minute. Regain your composure. I'll get your pill."

He put his hand up in the air to stop her. "Now listen carefully, Miss Byington. I would like you to move out of my way. Go over to your desk and do some filing or make some calls or do something. But, most of all, do these two things: get out of my way, and keep an eye out in case Gleason comes back. I'm going into the dungeon to see Gordon."

27

"Gordon!"

Gordon, Eve and Donald all turned their heads in unison toward the steps. They all knew the voice and they were all terrified.

"Listen, Chief," Gordon started babbling, but he was not to be heard. Eve and Donald both started in at the same time, offering defense for Gordon and pleading for mercy.

"BE QUIET!" Mitchell's booming voice again stopped them all in their tracks. He descended off the last step into the dungeon. As he came out of the shadows, he looked less threatening. His face was still red but the fire was gone from his eyes. In its place was a look of steely determination.

"Just let me speak. I'm going to have to now... before you disappear again, or get arrested, or murdered or something – all items that are secondary to me. I have a newspaper to run and you, Gordon Radits, are making that an increasingly difficult task for me. I have a good mind to fire you. Well, I'm sure everyone would say I've had a good mind to fire you almost every day since you started here. The problem is, you're a pretty darn good reporter. Sports, you usually just need the score and who scored what and when and a little color. But you have a knack for making it a story. Now, that alone is not enough to keep me from firing you. But this mess you left on my desk yesterday that was supposed to be the piece on the Princeton-Yale game! I say 'supposed to be' because I don't think you have the faintest clue that you gave me one-third of that story, one-third on some word "dord" or something – I can't make heads nor tails out of it – and one-third on that Nazi Bund piece. Now that Bund story. I ended up reading that three times. It's good. Really good. So, I want you to go back and finish that story. Make it big. Maybe we'll run it in a series. A whole week maybe. Get on it right away."

Gordon and Eve were both dumbstruck, but beaming at the praise. This was a major step up from the lowly sports beat.

"Thanks, Chief!" Gordon said. "But...."

"But what?"

"Uh. Eve is wanted for murder."

"What's your point?"

"Uh, and I'm wanted by the police."

"I just threw Gleason off the scent here. They're not

going to come back to look for either of you in this building."

"But still," Gordon insisted, "I can't work on another story no matter how important it is while my girlfriend is accused of murder."

"Well," Mitchell threw up his hands. "What do you want me to do about that?"

"Let me work on this. Let me find the real killer. An exclusive for The Topic. And we clear Eve at the same time. And then I'll do the best story you've ever seen on the Bund. How's that sound?"

"Fine, fine," Mitchell agreed. "Just get it done. No getting side-tracked. No new inventions. Just the story. Agreed?"

"Agreed, Chief." Gordon went over to shake Mitchell's hand, but he was already on his way up the stairs. He turned long enough to ask, "and just for my own piece of mind, what in God's name is a dord anyway?"

"Well, it's officially a word, but it's not really a word. You see, it was supposed to be a question…." Gordon was meandering through his explanation and Mitchell just didn't have the patience.

"Sorry I asked. Tell me later. Just get to work. You go clear Eve right this minute." He disappeared up the stairs.

28

Sergeant Gleason peeked into the patrol car sitting across from 26 Witherspoon Street. Officer O'Malley was reading the latest Superman comic book while Officer Pendleton was fast asleep in the driver's seat.

"What in blazes is going on here?" Gleason demanded.

"You were supposed to relieve Pendleton, not sing him a lullaby and put him to sleep." Pendleton was snoring away, a deep resonant tune that kept interrupting O'Malley's concentration on the comic book.

"Listen, Sergeant, I tried waking him up but it's like trying to stop a moving freight train."

Gleason opened the passenger door. "Get out!" He motioned to O'Malley. Gleason slid into the seat, took a deep breath and yelled at the top of his lungs, "PEN-DEL-TON!"

Pendleton shot to attention. "Nothing to report, sir. No activity."

"No activity in your brain, Pendleton," Gleason growled. "Now come with me. We're going to go interview Mr. Zucco."

O'Malley took over the driver's seat, Superman stuck inside his uniform pocket. Gleason and Pendleton headed up Witherspoon and went inside the bakery. A bell clanged as they shut the front door. Hillary Brooke stood up from behind the counter, holding a baking sheet full of apple danish. "May I help you?" the attractive saleswoman asked.

"Sergeant Gleason, ma'am," the detective said introducing himself. "This is Officer Pendleton. We'd like to speak to your boss about the murder that took place last night behind your building."

Miss Brooke was wearing an opened white baker's jacket over what appeared to be an expensive green dress with gold trim. She nervously straightened her uniform. "How awful," she said in a dry tone, "that poor fellow."

"Did you know him, Miss.... I'm sorry, I didn't catch your name."

"Hillary Brooke. I just work here part time, helping my fiance, Mr. Zucco when he's short-staffed. But no, I didn't know the man. Who was he, if I might ask?"

"That's what we're trying to find out, ma'am."

"Geez, it smells good in here," Pendleton sighed. He picked up a hot cross bun that was in a tray on top of a glass display case. "Do ya mind?" he asked, the food halfway into his mouth.

"No, of course not, officer," she said. "You go right ahead. We just baked them twenty minutes ago. Would you like one, Sergeant?"

"No thanks, Miss Brooke. Trying to watch the old waistline, you know. Now, I'm sorry, but is Mr. Zucco here?"

"Yes, I am here," said a man emerging from a door leading to the baking area. George Zucco was a medium built man with dark deep-set eyes and a very somber appearance. Like his fiancee, he was dressed both formally and for his particular profession. Underneath a full length white smock, he was wearing a gray business suit and black tie. "I assume you are here about the unfortunate problem behind my building."

"That is correct, sir. If you don't mind, could we have a few words with you?" Gleason asked.

"A few words? Or would you prefer details as to what I know about the incident?" Zucco replied.

Gleason immediately didn't like Zucco. "Whatever information you can provide us with will be very much appreciated," he said through gritted teeth.

"If you don't mind, can we conduct this meeting back here…" Zucco opened the door to lead the policemen off of the sales floor. Gleason accepted and made his way into the baking area. Pendleton followed directly behind, licking his fingers after finishing his treat.

"Did you enjoy our hot cross buns, officer?" Zucco asked, staring at the bits of frosting stuck on Pendleton's shirt collar.

"De-licious." Pendleton's tongue ran along his upper lip.

"They normally sell for three cents," Zucco mentioned, closing the door behind him. "Now, how can I help you gentlemen?"

"Well, first of all, did you see the murder take place? See anything suspicious around the time of the murder?"

"Now how would I have seen the murder, Sergeant? My fiancee and I were dining alone on the terrace at my home, which is over twenty miles from here. How far exactly do you think we can see from that terrace?" Zucco's tone was distinctly condescending.

"Now don't get uppity, mister. These are just questions we need to ask."

"I thought… isn't it standard police talk to say something like, 'Where were you on the night of the 19th at 10 p.m.?' Wouldn't that have been a more precise initial question?" Zucco turned to Pendleton. "Where were you last night around midnight?"

"Um, well," Pendleton was caught off guard. "I was guarding the entrance to the…."

"Wait a second," Gleason cut in, "we're here to interview you, Mr. Zucco."

"Very well." Zucco nodded without any emotion. "What is it you would like to know?"

"Just tell us everything you might know about the incident last night."

"There's very little I can tell you that would help, Sergeant. Hillary and I closed up the shop around eight o'clock, drove to my home and had a quiet dinner. I knew nothing about this sordid business until I got the phone call four o'clock this morning, telling me there was a dead body outside my back door. I arrived here around five forty-five and they asked me to identify the body. That coroner of yours, what's his name? Oh yes, Bore. Very impertinent fellow. I had never seen the victim before. No recollection at all and I stated so. That's all I can tell you. Now, are we done?"

Gleason had listened to the whole story and still didn't like the guy. He also did not completely believe his story. "I think we can leave it at that for now, Mr. Zucco. But just don't leave town without letting us know."

"But I live out of town. Do I need to call and inform you each night when I leave from work?" Zucco's sarcasm was straining the Sergeant's last nerve.

"Yes. As a matter of fact, that would be a great idea," he snapped, heading out to the front of the bakery. Pendleton followed behind, pausing to ask Miss Brooke if he might have another hot cross bun to take with him.

"Sure. How many would you like to order?" she said, moving over toward the cash register to ring up his sale. But Pendleton slapped at his pockets like he couldn't find any spare change and just said, "That's okay. I'll come back later."

Gleason was already making a note in his log book when Pendleton joined him on the street. "That Zucco guy ticks me off, Pendleton." He snapped, "We need to keep an eye on him."

"Gotcha, Chief." Pendleton replied.

29

From across the street a man called out for Sergeant Gleason. It was Walter Slezak, the butcher, standing in front of his shop. He waved for the detective to come over and stood there, his blood-soaked apron tied around his large waist, as shoppers passed him entering and exiting his store.

"Mr. Slezak, how are you?" Gleason extended his hand, "that sirloin the wife got from you last week was delicious. I can still taste it. My compliments."

"Compliments to your dear wife's cooking, I'm sure," the butcher replied. "Listen," he continued, "I just heard about these two murders and I was wondering if you've found the culprits?"

"No, not yet. But you have no need to worry."

"I hear you're looking for Gordon Radits. A suspect, I assume, or just a witness?"

"Sorry, Mr. Slezak, I'm not at liberty to discuss that. Let's just say I'm interested in speaking with the young man. Have you seen him?"

"No. No. Though he seemed such a nice boy. I was just concerned. You know, just normal curiosity."

"Well, if we find him, we'll get the word out. But, in the meantime, let us know if you do see him."

"Oh, I'll be sure to keep an eye out, Sergeant." Slezak emphasized, "I most certainly will."

As Gleason and Pendleton started back to their police car, Slezak called out, "We have some good rump roast coming in tomorrow, Sergeant. Send your wife over. I'll save a nice cut for you." Slezak watched as Gleason waved and then he went back into his butcher shop.

Slezak's shoes made a soft scraping sound as he walked over the sawdust that covered the floor. The chill that permeated the small shop always gave him a start when he entered the building, even after all these years in his chosen occupation. He went into the back room, where a diminutive man with slick black hair and enormous eyes was relishing his task of chopping a slab of beef into smaller portions with a huge red handled cleaver. Peter

Lorre stopped working long enough to listen as Slezak picked up the telephone and called The Topic.

"Miss Byington? This is Mr. Slezak calling again." He paused. "Oh, you haven't heard from Radits yet? You do still have my message for him? Yes, yes, Miss Byington. I'm sorry to keep calling. It's just that the information for the football game is time sensitive. I'm sure you would agree, what with the game just days away. I was beginning to worry about the story. Yes, yes. And Radits, too. He's not known to just vanish this way." Again, he paused, listening impatiently. "Thank you, Miss Byington. I do have complete faith that you will relay the message when he arrives. Thank you, again. Goodbye." He put down the phone and turned toward Lorre, seething.

"Peter! I do not like this at all. My attempt to lure Radits here with that story is just not working. We have to get him before it's too late."

Lorre gave him a wry smile.

"Peter, my friend, I trust you implicitly when it comes to finding people. You have such a knack for that task. I think I shall let you leave work early tonight...shall we say at dark? Maybe you can get some fresh air. Sounds good, my friend?" He gave Lorre a last devilish look, patting his hand lightly – the one holding the meat cleaver. He then returned to the front counter to greet his customers.

Lorre went back to his carving, feeling content with the pleasant assignment ahead of him.

30

It looked like some kind of monster: a short body with legs bowed, no head, arms wrapped around a massive torso made up of old newspapers. It was Donald Meek, bringing another stack from the archives over to a table where Gordon and Eve were deeply absorbed in past issues of The Topic. Meek knew the dungeon by heart and even without the benefit of an unobstructed view, he plopped the six month period from January through June 1938 right in the middle of the table without incident.

Eve had reasoned that they were going to be limited in their ability to go about town and all of them recalled various mentions of the Menjous in The Topic. They decided to start there, looking for any clue to jump start their investigation.

"Around the Town – Dinner with Monty" was a great source for local gossip that Eve thought might lead to something. Written by acid-tongued Monty Wooley, it often contained potentially libelous slander that should never have seen the light of day. Yet, despite the fact that Grant Mitchell bristled at the very mention of Wooley's name, his column got ever greater prominence in the paper. Mitchell would authorize pieces by the acerbic Wooley that came in too late, too long, or were filled with personal diatribes against someone who wouldn't give Wooley the time of day. The rumor going around the office was that Wooley actually had some sort of dirt on Mitchell and that was what was keeping him in print.

"Oh my gosh," Eve said, "will you look at this."

Gordon looked over from his stack of papers.

"Do you remember the tweed jacket everyone was wearing last winter?" Gordon and Donald shook their heads indicating they did not. "Here's an advertisement for it. I remember going to Gimbel's specifically for this jacket. It's the same one Jean Arthur was wearing in 'You Can't Take It With You.' You know, when she's Jimmy Stewart's secretary? I recall walking in the door at Gimbel's and bumping into a girl wearing that exact jacket. Then I took the escalator up to the second floor and there, going down the escalator, was the identical tweed jacket on another girl. By the time I reached the Women's Department, the girl behind the counter was wearing the exact same one. I decided then and there not to buy one. Yes, that's right. You know that nice navy dress with the gray buttons that I wear – the one that fits me so nicely? Well, I bought that instead."

"Uh, yes. Why, of course," Gordon replied, rolling his eyes. "In fact, that navy dress might just be the clue we need to clear you of this murder charge."

Eve slapped his shoulder. "Oh, I'm sorry. I'll get back to work."

They both dug into the task, scanning each page of the paper, start to finish and then laying the completed issues in a neat pile on the floor. After a couple hours, the stack was turning their hands black with the bleeding ink from flipping page after page of newsprint. Their eyes were beginning to feel the strain.

"This is going to take a lot more effort than we thought," Eve complained, stopping to rub her eyes and leaving dark circles that gave her face an eerie tiredness.

Gordon looked at his watch. "Why don't you take a little break to freshen up and then hit the next stack. In the meantime, I'll run over to the switchboard and see if I can find out who called Menjou yesterday."

"Only if you promise to be careful," she agreed.

Gordon gave her a quick, sweet kiss then headed for the steps. "Remember," he sang on his way up the stairs, "we solve this thing and then you have to agree to marry me, right?"

Before she had time to answer, he was up the steps and on his way out. Eve's eyes followed him up the stairs, catching a glimpse of something falling out of his pocket as he left. She ran over and picked it up. It was the piece of paper Gordon had pulled from the coat of the dead man in the alley. Neatly printed in a heavy handed penmanship was written:

40°44'34.089"N73°50'43.842"W

31

"Jeepers Creepers, where'd ya get those peepers. Jeepers Creepers, where'd ya get those eyes." The sound of Louie Armstrong's popular song echoed through the stairwell as Gordon climbed to the second floor of the Bell Telephone Company. The doors were propped open and the radio on the corner table was filling the room with music. In the middle of the room, Glenda Farrell sat in front of a battery of switchboard sockets. Her blonde hair was pulled back over her head and a headset circled over the top of her skull from one ear to the other.

"Gordy!" she blurted, spotting him coming through the open door. "You're sure in some hot water, ain't ya?"

"Sure am," he replied, "that's why I'm here. I need your help."

"Well, I really can't hide you anywhere, but you don't have to worry about me snitching to the cops on you." She was chomping away at a huge wad of chewing gum. "Hold on a second," she said, shifting to speak into the mouthpiece hanging from her neck. "Yes, ma'am. I'll connect you." She plugged a cord into one of the sockets on the switchboard. She turned her full attention back to Gordon. "Is Eve okay? Soon as I heard the news about the murder and all, I knew the two of you were innocent."

"Thanks. She's fine," Gordon smiled. "But you can really help us if you can remember one thing. There was a phone call made yesterday afternoon right before the murder took place. It was maybe around four o'clock. Someone telephoned Professor Menjou. We need to know who that was."

"Sure, honey, I remember that call like it just happened. You see, it was from Philadelphia. The long distance operator said, 'I've got a call for Professor Adolph Menjou from the Blue Pearl Hotel in Philadelphia.' I love blue pearls, so naturally it stuck in my head." Glenda surveyed her recent manicure before glancing up at Gordon.

"Did the person give a name?" Gordon asked.

"Nope. No name at all. I never heard the caller, only the operator asking me to put the call through."

"Can you do me a favor? Can you try calling them back to see if they can give you a name? Who made the call?"

"Sure. Anything for you and Eve, Gordy. Just give me a sec." She looked up some information and went about placing the call to Philadelphia.

Gordon wandered over to the second floor window and looked out over the street.

"Gordon," Glenda called. "Here you go. Not much I'm afraid. They say the name listed was Joe Smith. Good luck with that. They gave me his room number – 220 – but said him and the doll with him, a Mrs. Smith she called herself, checked out early this morning."

"Smith. Gee, that took imagination. Room 220? At the Blue Pearl? Well, thanks, Glenda. You're the best." Gordon headed down the stairs, trying to figure out his next move. Going to Philadelphia was a long shot, but it might be necessary. It was getting colder out and he pushed up his collar as he hurried down the tree-lined street.

Before long he sensed that someone was walking behind him. He slowed down to see if the person would pass, but his follower matched his pace. He decided to speed up, but just then he felt a sharp object being pressed into his back.

"Mr. Radits. I have a friend who would like to see you."

32

The second floor room was badly lit and sparsely furnished - just two hard-backed chairs facing a wooden desk. A shaded table lamp sat on the far corner of the desk. When Gordon was led into the room by Peter Lorre, Walter Slezak looked up from the desk and gave a wry smile.

"Gordon, I've been looking forward to meeting you. I've left message after message," he turned his palms upwards and shrugged his large shoulders, "but, alas, no luck. I am so glad you decided to visit."

"You know," Gordon replied, "I was just on my way over to the meat market to see you when your friend here redirected me. Some coincidence, huh?" For some reason even he couldn't fathom, Gordon was more annoyed than frightened.

Slezak's smile was chiseled into his face and his eyes were burning. He did not like Gordon, but was doing his best to maintain his composure. "Now, about this story," he started.

"Oh, the Princeton-Yale scoop? That's right. You had some inside information about the game that would be front page stuff…"

"That was just my humorous way of trying to meet you. Funny, don't you think?" There was a silent pause, then Slezak continued, "What I am most interested in is this Bund story you are writing…."

"Geez, I just got that assignment. It's very nearly top secret and yet you know about it? Maybe you should be the investigative reporter."

"I do not think flippancy suits you well, Mr. Radits. This is a matter of the utmost seriousness and I would hope we would both treat it as such." Peter Lorre moved out of the shadows behind Gordon and over next to Slezak. He took a seat on the end of the desk, his right hand carefully draped over his lap, prominently displaying a handgun. "You see, Gordon," Slezak continued, "I am, shall we say, a friend of the German-American Bund. I know the founders of the local group. I am personal friends with many of the members of the organization. They are all very proud of their German heritage, as well as their German citizenship. The years of degradation and embarrassment our people have had to endure since the end of the Great War, well, they have been almost too much to bear. Whether the grievances some have charged over the resurgence of our people has had any relevance is not for me to say. My foremost goal is to assure that our German-American community, as well as our Fatherland, continues to grow and prosper. Can you see where my concerns lie, Gordon?"

"Uh-huh," Gordon nodded. "Please continue."

"You will have to admit that there have been many scurrilous stories printed about the German-American Bund, some even referring to them as the Nazi Bund.

These stories have taken great liberties with the truth and, as a result, there is, I will admit, a growing reticence in America to accept the Bund as a legitimate organization. In the Princeton area, we have taken great pains to keep a low profile, to expand our group without the nonsense that the press so often provokes."

"So, if I understand correctly, you'd like me to kill this story?" Gordon asked.

"That would be a very pleasant outcome." There was just a hint of a genuine smile on Slezak's face. "But that would still be my second choice. You see, after all the work we have done, a positive story could do so much to reverse the negativity of the past. Do you see what I'm driving at? We have a parcel of land outside of the town – as you might very well know – that we have put much time, money and sweat into. We have introduced a camp where we instill a sense of pride in the next generation of German-Americans. We strengthen their bodies and their wills."

He continued, "What I am suggesting is that you concentrate on the positive aspects of the Bund. Show the way we have fashioned such an impressive group of youngsters who are polished and disciplined in their camp routines. And I am prepared to make it worth your while to write such a glowing narrative."

"Propaganda, you mean," Gordon shot back, then added, "Look. I'm a journalist at The Topic. I think you're looking for the advertising department. Third floor. Make a quick right."

Slezak slammed his fist on the desk. "This is not a joking matter, my boy." He signaled to Lorre, who seemed to savor the implied request. Lorre stood up and pointed the gun directly at Gordon's temple. In the quiet moment of the confrontation, Lorre emitted a barely detectable noise, not unlike the purr of a cat.

"It has been my intention," Slezak said, while starting to pace across the room, "to convince you through a rational argument why it is so important for this story to be positive in nature. I always regret when circumstances make it necessary for threats or the primitive use of physical violence to come into play. So, Radits, let me appeal one last time to your sense of responsibility. Let's remember that your story can cement the backward thinking of the general population or it can enlighten them about the true mission of the German-American Bund."

"You mean agree or get shot." Gordon boiled down the choices.

"Yes." Slezak affirmed.

"First of all," Gordon started, "I would have been very open to listening to your side of the issue and incorporating that into my final piece, but, you have to admit, trying to lure me to your office under false football pretenses and then forcing me here at the point of a knife are not a good start. You made some relevant points in your argument, I will admit, but to again demand – not request, not even 'please, will you' – but to demand under the threat of… I'm not sure… what's it going to be – just pain or maybe death – I think you may have just lost your argument."

For the first time, the sardonic smile on Slezak's face disappeared, replaced with hardly contained fury. "You refuse?"

"Look. I'm really, truly sorry. I'd love to write a nice fluff bio for the Bund, but no dice."

"That is too bad, my friend. You see, after this conversation we had it would not be wise for me to let you leave the room, unless you agreed to be on our side." He motioned to Lorre. "I'm sure you understand."

Gordon raised his hands signaling them to stop. "Sure, I understand. But I'd like you to understand something, too. I would not be speaking with such candor if I didn't feel I could leave here safely. You see, I have already done some research on the Bund. You know about this or you wouldn't have been so desperate to contact me. I have already handed a draft of that story in to the paper. And, my research included some juicy bits of detail about you, Mr. Slezak. So don't think I wasn't able to put two and two together when you kept leaving messages for me at The Topic. I knew you were scared about this story. Just from what I've learned about you, I knew that this," and he pointed his head toward Peter Lorre, "might be your idea of resolution. So, I prepared a little insurance policy, Mr. Slezak. I wrote an addendum to my story detailing your phone calls and your history and I'm sure that if anything happens to me, the police will also be able to put two and two together. I have made it very clear that if I'm found dead, that extra piece will get published."

Slezak and Lorre stood frozen, apparently unprepared for this development.

"Now, I'm going to walk out of this room." Gordon slowly backed up toward the door. "And if you know what's good for you, don't bother me again." He pulled the door closed, Slezak's frozen blank stare forever in his memory. His hand was shaking as he used it to guide himself along the banister down the dark stairway and out of the building.

He rushed off down the street. He could not comprehend how, while having a gun pointed at him for the first time in his life, he had been able to concoct such a story. Not only was he able to deliver it without fumbling, but they actually fell for it.

33

"I don't believe him." Slezak was furious. "That story was nonsense."

"Then why didn't you let me stop him, boss. If what he said was not true, why did we let him slip right through our fingers?" Lorre asked.

"I don't believe him, but I'm not sure. Not one hundred percent sure. And all it takes is that one percent to ruin everything I've worked for," Slezak responded.

"But letting him go after threatening him makes it one hundred percent positive that he'll print those charges against you, doesn't it?" Lorre didn't understand Slezak's logic.

"Ever play with matches, Peter?" Slezak inquired of his assistant.

Lorre nodded affirmatively, still unclear of the plan.

"My dear Mr. Lorre. If there is, shall we say, an 'accident' at the Topic offices and everything in it burns to the ground, all the stories that are to be printed will be reduced to cinders. Yes? Then our good Mr. Radits has nothing to hold over our heads anymore, does he? And then, then we can eliminate him. One hundred percent dead, see?"

"Oh, yes. Yes indeed." Lorre nearly smacked his lips, salivating over the prospects of his upcoming deeds.

"There is a large can of kerosene down in the cellar of this building. Take that and some matches and stake out The Topic until everyone leaves for the night. Torch it, and then kill Gordon Radits."

34

The door was open no more than two inches and Edna May Oliver's eyes were darting back and forth, scouring the corridor outside her apartment. She was certain she had heard the crackling linoleum under someone's careful footsteps. But there was no movement. Her gaze rested on a shadow. Maybe her eyes were playing tricks on her, but the more she concentrated, the more it seemed like a woman in an overcoat was pressed against the wall. A hissing sound from behind her forced Edna May to shut the door and trace the noise to its source. A large pot on her stove was boiling over and the steaming liquid was leaping off the edge of the pot, yelling for her to turn down the flame. She shut the burner off. It's done, she thought. Some hot soup, just what Gordon and Eve could use. She went into her kitchen closet and picked out a bigger picnic basket than the one she had used just that morning. She covered the pot and placed it in the basket along with bowls, spoons and napkins. She placed two fresh loaves of homemade bread alongside the pot to keep it from moving in the basket. She was just about to cover up the feast when she recalled how much Eve loved chocolate. She went to her pantry and took out a foil-wrapped chocolate bar she had been saving for herself. She carefully added it to the far end of the basket, away from the heat of the soup pot.

Edna May cracked the door slightly to peek outside before opening it wide enough to leave. She had hoped she could spot the person in the shadow before leaving, but now the hallway was empty. She locked her door and hurried down the stairs. She would make sure that poor couple had some good nourishment before she headed over to see Sergeant Gleason.

The two of them shared a history from many, many years ago. James Gleason had just started on the force, and Edna May was a kindergarten teacher at a private girl's school where property theft had reached epidemic proportions. It was Edna May who had maneuvered the rough-at-the-edges officer around the scared young schoolgirls and who helped to uncover some of the clues that eventually led to the solving of the crimes. James Gleason got all the credit, but he reluctantly admitted that Edna May's help had made all the difference, and he treated her opinions on such matters in high regard ever since.

In this case, she had plenty to say to Detective Sergeant Gleason about Mr. Kibbee, in particular, as well as some of the other lodgers at 26 Witherspoon Street.

35

Edna May entered The Topic building and greeted Miss Byington, who said with a wink and a hint of good-natured fun, "I guess that's another basketful of goodies for your dear friend, Mr. Meek."

"Very perceptive, my dear. Mr. Meek just adores my cooking." Edna May happily joined in on the joke and proceeded down into the dungeon. There she found Gordon, Eve and Donald all huddled together on the floor concentrating on something in front of them. "Either you've been fooling around with that football contraption again or you knew I was coming with the basket and got yourselves in a picnic mood." She held the basket up for them to see. It was obviously too heavy for her to lift, and so Gordon jumped up to take it from her.

"Ah, another banquet from our favorite chef," he beamed, sniffing the aroma from underneath the basket's covering.

They all took a bowl of hot soup and some bread. A chair was pulled up for Miss Oliver so she could see what was going on down on the floor. Eve was sitting on the floor in front of an open map of Princeton and the vicinity. It was an old map, the creases from where it had been folded and unfolded creating little tears in the paper, turning 'Plainsboro" into 'ainsboro.' But, as Eve said, it was functional.

"First," she started to explain to Edna May, "a lot has happened, but we don't seem to have made too much progress. We've gone through three years of The Topic. There were a few mentions of Professor Menjou, and an enormous amount for his wife, but they were all innocuous items – a bridge get-together, a luncheon to benefit the church, things like that. A dead end, so far. Gordon checked with Glenda about the phone call to the Professor right before he was killed. The call came from a hotel in Philadelphia. A Mr. and Mrs. Smith. No other details. No forwarding address. And as if we're not having enough to do with this, Gordon got threatened by Mr. Slezak while he was on his way back here."

"Mr. Slezak? The butcher?" Edna May cut in. "Why in heaven's name would he threaten Gordon?"

"Well," Eve explained, "Mr. Slezak has some interest in that German-American society. You know, that group that was meeting down in the community room in the library. Anyway, he must take it pretty seriously. He had that fellow that works in the butcher shop…."

"Oh, I know who you mean. The one with the bug eyes. He gives me the heebie-jeebies."

"Yes. Exactly."

"If he's waiting on me, I just get so unsettled. He just stares at the meat – intensely – before he wraps it up."

"Yes, I noticed the same thing!"

"What did you say his name is?"

"It's Lorre. Peter Lorre. He had a gun pointed right at Gordon. And if it wasn't for some quick thinking, Gordon might not be here." Eve lovingly patted Gordon's hand. "Anyway, that is another worry to add to the bundle. But, what we've all decided is that Gordon and I should get out of town and go to that hotel in Philadelphia. We thought maybe talking to the staff there... in person... well, we might be able to get some details, some clues."

"All well and good," Edna May agreed, "but how are you going to get out of town? The police have check points at every single road out of Princeton."

"Yes, Donald told us about that when he came back from some errands. That's what this map is for. We were plotting..." Eve paused for effect, "...our escape." She pointed down at the map, making sure everyone was following along. "Look. Donald has already taken the canoe and placed it behind a row of mums in Mr. Mitchell's backyard. His yard is just thirty-seven feet from this little jutting out point on Lake Carnegie. At nine o'clock, Donald leaves the building, closes up and walks up Nassau Street. If he sees any police watching the building, he will go back in, like he forgot something. That's our sign that it's not safe. If after four minutes he hasn't returned, we know the coast is clear. We exit through the back door, proceed one hundred and fifty feet south through these three yards. Then we follow this path," she pointed to a spot on the map and then moved her finger along various roads and alleyways until she stopped at Mr. Mitchell's residence. We quietly put the canoe in the lake and then float north, up to this point. This is well beyond the city limits. This is a wonderful area, easy to hide the canoe and a car. That's where Donald has parked his Cadillac and," she pulled from her pocket a single silver key tied to a small circle of twine, "we are ready to go. We get in, clear of the roadblocks, and head right into Philly."

"Eve, that's an amazing plan," Edna May said. "I hope it works. If there's any way I can help, I want to know."

"Your feeding us and being on our side has meant more to us than you can imagine," Gordon piped in.

"Oh, that's nothing. You know, I can be a pretty fair detective if I put my mind to it, so…."

"As a matter of fact," Eve offered, "were you able to see if my parents were back yet?"

"Now this is strange in its own right," Edna May stated. "I have been watching for them every minute that I've been home. I haven't seen them come in. I've even looked late at night. I went down to the street and looked up at the windows, but no lights, just pitch black. And I know that when they do their little trips to the beach they're usually back by the next morning, or by two o'clock at the latest. I hate to say this, but something's just not right. I'm sure of it."

She asked Eve, "Can you try calling them? Maybe they're having such a good time they decided to extend their stay?"

"No," Eve explained, "it's just a little bungalow near the beach. There was a phone there, but a few months ago the phone service stopped working. Dad said some summer storms had knocked out the power lines and since the cottage was so isolated they just had to wait until the local phone company got around to repairing it. Gee, I just don't know what to do now. What if something happened to them? I mean, the car, my dad's not such a good driver.

I don't even know if they got there okay."

Gordon could see the worry in Eve's face. "I know," he suggested, "we can just make a slight detour."

"A detour? What are you talking about?" Eve was obviously puzzled.

"First, we make our escape. Then we take Donald's car and head to Philly…by way of Atlantic City!"

"Would that actually work?" she asked.

"Of course," he confidently replied. "In fact, the timing works out even better. We will get into Atlantic City just after midnight. We check on your parents, make sure they're okay. Maybe your mom can even give me a nice plate of her rolled meat and cabbage, if she has any handy. We get an hour or two to rest and then we get to Philly first thing in the morning. It would be right when the people working at the hotel would all be in. If we went there straight away tonight, most of them would be gone for the evening."

"It does seem to make sense," Eve agreed, as did Donald and Edna May.

"The car has a full tank of gas," Donald added. "You should be able to make the whole trip without having to refill."

Eve was anxious to get started. It was almost time. They finished up their food, and Eve got giddy as Edna May broke out the chocolate bar. As she folded up the map, Eve announced, "Okay. Let's go."

36

Donald Meek buttoned up his camel hair overcoat. It was too big for him and made him look even tinier than he was. He turned out the last light at The Topic building and locked the door. He went to drop off a bag full of trash in a bin on the side of the building, all the while scanning the perimeter of the building for any spying policemen. He saw a woman walking a frantic Wire Fox Terrier, and he immediately recognized her as Myrna Loy, a local woman. They waved politely to each other and continued on their separate ways. As Donald turned to head up Nassau Street, his eyes kept darting back and forth for any movement.

Exactly four minutes later, the knob on the door to the rear exit of The Topic building slowly turned to open. As the two figures moved quickly through the darkness in their journey toward the lake, a small black car pulled down the side street just behind them. The car had its lights off, so Gordon and Eve did not notice it. But the little man with the great big eyes in the driver's seat noticed them.

37

Peter Lorre looked down at the tin of kerosene sitting next to him. The building would have to wait a few minutes. His instructions were to torch the building, then kill Radits. Lorre smirked. What would Slezak think. Here he was, thinking for himself, a simple efficient reversal in order and the plan would still be complete. Kill Gordon first and then return to burn down The Topic building. He made sure his gun was in his coat pocket and then he quickly got out of the car and carefully trailed his target and his girlfriend through the yards of the local residents. Lorre stayed back far enough so he would not be seen, but close enough to keep them in sight. He was in no hurry, waiting until they were away from homes where he could not be spotted after the killings.

When their winding path led to a two-story colonial home on a tree-lined cul-de-sac, Lorre thought he might have the perfect setting to complete his job. The closed drapes and unlit windows gave him no reason to think otherwise. He was, however, unaware that it was Grant Mitchell's home. He decided to circle around from the other side of the house to get a clear unobstructed view. He put his hand in his right jacket pocket and kept it clutched to his revolver as he stealthily moved through the brush.

When he reached the back of the house, he was alarmed to see Gordon and Eve sprinting away into the woods, each grasping the side of a gray canoe. He immediately dashed off into the woods after them. At one point, he pulled the gun from his jacket and aimed at a tree trunk he had just passed. He put the gun back though, and gave a low chuckle as a black squirrel scurried up the tree trunk. He turned and hurried on, getting anxious to end the hunt.

38

The water glistened on Lake Carnegie, flowing along the northeastern outskirts of Princeton. The canoe quietly cut through the water, heading north toward the Millstone River. Gordon and Eve sat low inside the canoe trying to be as quiet and inconspicuous as possible, even as they remained the lone visible objects in the water.

There were thousands of stars out in the clear cold

evening. Eve was getting chilly, but the brisk air was invigorating. "If we weren't stuck in the middle of a murder, this would really be the bees knees. You know, boating under the stars. A lake all to ourselves." She began to very softly hum the tune, "Moonlight Serenade."

But Gordon, not one to let an opportunity pass by, broke into her song with a different Glenn Miller song, "Tell me it's true love. Say you'll be mine when the moon disappears." He couldn't remember all the lyrics so he simply repeated the lines.

"Shhh." Eve tried to quiet him down, looking both ways as if his crooning had attracted attention on both sides of the lake. This only spurred him on more. He stood up in the canoe, his feet straddling both sides as it wobbled a bit from his movement.

"All right, Eve," Gordon whispered. "I am going to start singing at the top of my lungs, the echoes of my voice will ripple across the whole region unless you answer me right now. Will you marry me?"

He knew it wasn't right to force her to respond by threat, but he was inspired by the moment and the moonlight. The lake was completely silent. Gordon waited for Eve's answer. Eve thought how crazy he was and the boat rocked slightly back and forth.

Then a gunshot rang out. Gordon fell forward, his chin slammed into Eve's knee. They both groaned in pain.

"Gordon!" she screamed. "Are you all right?"

"Yeah." He fumbled with the words. "Just proves you 'kneed' me."

"Ha-ha. Very funny. No. I mean… were you shot?"

"I don't think so. Although I think I felt a bullet whizz right by me." He pressed his hand down on her back. "Stay down. We don't know who did that or where they are. It's not likely that they're done."

Just then another shot rang out, appearing to come from a wooded area near the shoreline. They couldn't see anything at all, but they could hear the distinct sound of someone or something falling to the ground. Then the rustle of leaves as footsteps marched off into the distance.

Eve and Gordon could not see the body of Peter Lorre laying face down in a thicket of branches, nor could they see the person who had just killed him quietly making his way back to Princeton.

39

Gordon and Eve could make no sense out of the gunshots on the lake. They stayed down as low as they could in the canoe, while frantically rowing their way to their rendezvous point. With arms and shoulders aching from the pace of rowing, they pulled the canoe ashore, hid it, and went to the clearing where they found Donald Meek's car.

It was a monster of a car – a 1935 Cadillac Twelve Town Car. The shiny chrome details highlighted the sleek black exterior of the auto. A luxury vehicle was certainly beyond the means of Donald Meek. It had originally been purchased by Grant Mitchell, but the newspaper mogul had no patience for anything at all, let alone an automobile that wouldn't always start properly, or one that would decide to have a pouting fit in the middle of a busy intersection. So, after one frustrating hot summer afternoon spent parked in the middle of the intersection of Nassau and Witherspoon, Mitchell reached his boiling point. He left the car right in the midst of traffic, leaving fellow motorists beeping and yelling at him. He stormed into The Topic building and offered the car for free to anyone who would go retrieve it. Donald Meek, being the only one in the office at the time, won by process of elimination.

Naturally, the sight of this little man trying in vain to push the gargantuan car prompted some fifteen passersby to stop and help him push the car all the way back to The Topic building. Gordon had just returned from an assignment on a Trenton Senators game when he saw the mass of people crowded around the car. After Donald filled him in on the situation, Gordon pulled open the hood, rolled off some technical mumbo jumbo under his breath, added an "A-ha" and later that night, with Meek holding a flashlight pointed under the hood, Gordon proclaimed the problem solved. Mitchell was furious that Gordon missed the deadline again for his story. But a further irritant was the image of the tiny Donald Meek behind the steering wheel of this elegant oversized vehicle that only a fraction of the American public could afford.

The first thing Gordon and Eve noticed when they got in the car was a small basket of fruits and chocolate. A note that read "Good Luck" was pinned to an apple. Edna May Oliver, they fondly thought. Gordon slipped the car into gear and they headed off toward Atlantic City.

40

Edna May Oliver marched up the steps and into the Princeton Police Department. Despite the fact that there was no sign of rain in sight, she carried at her side an orange and black striped umbrella. Orange and black were the official colors of Princeton University, but Edna May wasn't carrying it for show or for inclement weather but as protection. The police department, she had discovered previously, was a very dangerous place. Officer Pendleton, in particular, had a habit of tripping over things whenever he was in her company. Invariably, he'd bump into her and knock things over on top of her in the process. Sergeant Gleason claimed it was because she berated him every time she saw him, which resulted in his becoming unsettled and nervous to the point that he became all thumbs. Edna May dismissed this reasoning, claiming Pendleton was just "a clumsy dunce." Her pre-emptive strategy was to whack him with the umbrella anytime he came within tripping distance, thereby scaring him away and preventing potential disasters.

This particular umbrella had also come in handy the previous summer when she was trying to enter the station, only to be accosted by two drunkards. Charlie Ruggles and Walter Catlett, both dressed in tails and top hats, were attempting to escape from a disorderly conduct charge by running out the front door as Officer O'Malley was lugging them into the station. Unfortunately, they both got stuck in the door frame. They were arguing, laughing themselves silly and, after freeing themselves but not being able to walk straight, they crashed right into Edna May. Both started to profusely apologize, but she whisked out her umbrella and started whacking the two of them across their backs anyway. "Go away! Go away!" she yelled at them. "You pair of filthy no-good…" and her voice trailed off.

O'Malley had rushed over and led them back to be locked up. "Is that weapon registered?" he sternly asked Edna May as he led them into the building.

Sergeant Gleason's feet were up on the desk when Edna May barged in. The stare she gave to his shoes was effective and he was quickly sitting straight up in his desk chair, feet firmly on the floor. "Edna May. So nice to see you," he said. "What brings you to the police station? Stray cat on the loose? Pickles overpriced at Bailey's grocery store?"

"I'm here on serious business, James." She was not smiling. "It's high time you took this Menjou case seriously."

That got Gleason's Irish blood boiling. His jaw tightened and his eyebrows repositioned themselves into angry lines. "Edna May. I've been on that case twenty hours a day. You might think shoes up on a desk means loafing, but for me it means thinking." He pointed with his right finger up to the top of his head. "Right up here. The gears are turning and I'm putting all the pieces together. We haven't picked up Eve yet, or Gordon, but believe me, I've got this thing under control."

"Well, maybe the gears up there need some oil," she gave him a disgusted look, "if you think Gordon or Eve had anything to do with that murder. You're plain old loopy!"

"Now, Edna May. Don't go…."

"Don't give me that 'Now, Edna May' stuff," she pulled up a chair and sat directly across from him at his desk. "I need to fill you in on some facts your crackpot detectives know nothing about." James Gleason knew Edna May Oliver all too well to argue. He sat back and listened.

41

"No, no. I think you make a left up here," Eve

sounded unsure. "Oh, I just can't remember. Everything looks so different. It has to be at least two years since I came down to the bungalow with them. I know I should have come more often, but with school and work, well, you know, it just never worked out."

Gordon pulled the car to the side of the road. "Look, just relax and think back. Maybe some landmarks might jog your memory."

"I know. But all these bungalows look so different now." She pointed toward a row of buildings with peeling paint, debris scattered in the yards and boarded up windows. "Hmmm. You know what? I said the road was about two hundred yards from that farm stand, but I'm trying to picture it in my head. It WAS different the last time. I think maybe they moved the stand up the road more. That would mean we need to go maybe another forty yards."

Gordon pulled the car back onto the dirt road and proceeded, going as slowly as possible so Eve could get her bearings.

"That's it! There it is!" she exclaimed, pointing toward a narrow street running behind a pale green bungalow.

Gordon shut off the headlights and drove forward. The little cottages became more sparse as they continued. After a mile, it got to the point where only one building was visible. They passed by that one, Eve shaking her head but insisting that they were headed in the right direction. They could hear the nearby roar of the Atlantic Ocean and they both realized they would soon run out of road.

"That's it!" Eve said as a small dark square building came into view. The car rumbled over gravel and sand and finally stopped directly in front of the door. There was no sign of any occupants. It was completely dark. "My gosh.

It doesn't look like they're here," Eve said, barely whispering.

"Maybe they're sleeping?" Gordon tried to reason.

"I don't know. I don't see their car. I don't see any lights at all." Eve went up and knocked on the door while Gordon peered inside a front window. She knocked again, but there was no sound, no movement. "What shall we do?" she asked.

Gordon turned the doorknob, but it was locked. He pushed his shoulder up against the door to force it open, but only groaned as the door did more damage to his shoulder than he did to the door. He picked up a golf ball-sized stone from the sand and broke the glass on the window. He had to hit it again to make it wide enough to reach in and unlock the window. "Uh, sorry about that," he apologized to Eve.

"What? What's wrong?"

"Um. The window wasn't locked."

"Gordon, I will be sending you a bill for new glass panes." She punched him. "Come on, climb in."

He pulled open the window, brushed the glass shards off of the sill and climbed into the room. Feeling around in the dark, he made his way to the door and opened it to let Eve in. They flicked the light switch, but there was no power. Gordon went out to the car and grabbed a flashlight. It was still too dark to see much so they used the flashlight to go through the cupboards until they found a small oil lamp. When they placed it on the table in the middle of the room, it lit up the whole area, flickering slightly but telling the story they needed to know.

No one had been there for quite some time. Dust covered everything.

"How can this be?" Eve wondered. "They've been taking weekend trips here for the last three months.

There's no way they've been here in at least a year from the looks of it. I just don't understand." She strolled across the room, picked up a cup or plate here or there, and seeing dust covering it, placed it right back down.

Gordon looked in the bathroom and checked the bedrooms. "It looks like they went through and cleared almost everything out the last time they were here. Wait. What's this?" He crouched down at the fireplace. "It looks like someone was burning some papers. Look at this charred newsprint." He stuck his hand into the fireplace and pulled down a few pages that were stuck to the flue that had not been completely burned. The first was a map of the United States, totally destroyed except for the eastern seaboard of New England with stray pencil markings from Portland, Maine to Boston. "Oh my gosh!" Gordon yelled as he uncovered the next piece of debris. It was part of a newspaper article with a picture of six men at some sort of ceremony. Two of the men in the picture were very familiar. One was Professor Adolph Menjou. The other was Eve's father, Karl Krell.

42

"What!" Eve shouted from one of the bedrooms.

"Were your father and Professor Menjou friends?"

"Not that I know of," she said, coming into the room. "They knew each other to say hello, but as far as I know, that's it."

"Well, you better look at this," he said, pushing the tattered photo in front of her. "This looks like an old picture. They both still had a full head of hair," Gordon was doing his best Sherlock Holmes imitation. "This is definitely from a newspaper, but the specifics are vague. Looks like it's the something Times. And the date is March 31, 191-, the last digit is missing. Looks like it could be the New York Times, but anywhere from 1910 to 1919. Eve, do you recognize any of the other men in this photo?"

"Hmmm." She held the clipping up to the light, but then shook her head. "Nope. Why would it be in the fireplace? Why would it be here, in the bungalow? It doesn't make any sense at all. Was there anything else in the fireplace?" she asked. He showed her the only other piece of paper - the map, which didn't offer any clues, either. After thoroughly searching the rest of the bungalow, they decided that they would just continue on to Philadelphia.

The trek was a long one, going all the way across the state of New Jersey into Pennsylvania. They decided to stop at "Bert's All Nit Diner," whose outside lights were all flickering like they were ready to go out at any second. The "e" in "Nite" had already bitten the dust. The parking lot was empty but Gordon and Eve needed coffee and a place where they could make a phone call, so they pulled in.

Gloria Stuart was the bleary-eyed blonde waitress that slid two cups of hot coffee onto the table at the booth in which they were sitting. She told them the public phone was out of order, but when she saw how distressed they were, she offered to let them use the diner telephone – if they made it quick before her boss returned.

Eve rang Edna May's phone number. "I'm sorry to call you at this time of night, Miss Oliver, but we just left the bungalow. My parents hadn't been there, and we don't know who else to turn to."

"Pooh, pooh, dear," Edna May's sleepy voice was

reassuring, "I'm here to help any way I can."

Eve quickly detailed the results of their search of the bungalow. "This picture might lead us in the right direction, but we need more information. If you can go to the library and try to locate the whole article, and, I don't know if she'll even talk to you, but if you can call Mrs. Menjou and see if she recalls the event. I don't know what else to say. If you find out any news, call the Blue Pearl Hotel in Philadelphia and leave a message at the front desk. We'll call you when we arrive."

"Now, don't you worry, dear. I'll take care of it." Edna May hung up. Then she picked up the receiver and dialed the number written on a piece of paper right next to her telephone.

43

Gloria Stuart strolled over and refilled their coffee cups, then went back to sweeping the floor behind the counter. Her mind drifted as she created a tidy pile of toast crumbs, squashed peas and carrots, and broken sugar cubes. The textbooks under the counter kept beckoning her. She knew she had to get her studying done while there was a lull in traffic, but she was so tired from working the graveyard shift at the diner that she couldn't get any school work done. The diner's business was dwindling anyway and it was probably best if she quit, but she wasn't the type of person that could desert a sinking ship.

She put down the broom and went over to a circular display in the corner. She removed two stale glazed donuts from under a clear glass cover and placed them on a paper doily on a plate. "On the house," she said to Eve and

Gordon as she topped off their coffee again. "Poor kids," she thought. They looked like they'd had a pretty rough day. She gave them a soft smile and left them alone. It turned out that Bert's was just what they needed to get themselves back on the road.

44

It was early morning when they arrived in Philadelphia. They drove along Third Street just parallel to the Delaware River until they passed Broad Street and found the Blue Pearl Hotel. Looking like an apartment building in slight disrepair, there was a small sign hanging over the main entrance proclaiming itself to truly be a hotel. The hustle and bustle of early morning activity was underway. Occupants were checking out. Attendants were servicing rooms. Guests were enjoying breakfast in the small dining area across from the front desk. To save time, Eve and Gordon decided to separate and question every employee they saw.

Gordon headed up to the second floor, Eve started out in the lobby. Nearly every worker she talked to was unable to place the occupants of Room 220. Except for one. The doorman immediately went into detail about a tall man, balding with white hair, who drove a big covered truck filled with apples. He said the man would always reach under the heavy black tarp that covered the truck and hand him a shiny red apple. The doorman described him as a fruit wholesaler who had stayed there frequently over the last four months. He could supply no other information, so Eve thanked him and headed for the café.

She took a seat and ordered two coffees and two

buttered rolls. She decided to take one up to Gordon after she questioned the waitress. Before she had a chance to take a sip of her coffee, Gordon showed up, looking white as a ghost.

"Here, have some coffee," Eve said, worried at Gordon's appearance. "What on earth is the matter?"

He sat down at the table, pushing the saucer aside. "I found the woman that cleans the rooms and she distinctly remembered the couple that stayed here."

"Oh," Eve said. "I found out about a truck that the man drove."

"Hmmm," Gordon mused, "this woman didn't mention the truck, but she recalled this couple coming for a day or two regularly over the last few months. She remembered them as a very courteous pair, but that they kept to themselves. She called them Mr. and Mr. Smith, and I knew that wasn't going to help us at all. She didn't recall any details of anything they said except for one mention of Plainsboro – because she has a cousin who lives there. Other than that, she said their conversations were limited to pleasantries – nice day, fine job on the sheets – but no other details."

He took a nibble from the buttered roll. "She described the man like this: tall, balding but with a little bit of white hair, a bit of a scar over his right eyebrow."

Eve's back straightened.

Gordon continued. "The woman was short and plump, with big thick glasses and a heavy accent, maybe Eastern European or Russian." He put his hand on top of Eve's, and with his other hand pulled out the tattered photo they had recovered from the bungalow fireplace. "I showed her this picture." He paused. "She identified your father as the man who called himself Mr. Smith."

45

"Let's see," Eve eventually replied. "In the last forty-eight hours I've been a witness to a murder, been accused of that murder, slept in a dungeon, had my boyfriend threatened and shot at, went on a wild goose chase… and now find out that my parents are leading a double life and lying to me about it! What's next? Maybe Martians really landing in Grover's Mills?"

"Yeah, in gigantic silver flying saucers," Gordon added.

"And, we'll be the only two humans they capture for their evil experiments back on Mars."

Just then they heard a bellhop announcing: "Telephone for Eve Krell. Paging Eve Krell. Telephone for Eve Krell."

Eve followed the young man to the front desk where she picked up the phone.

"Eve," an out-of-breath Edna May Oliver shouted into the phone, "I'm so glad I caught you there. I just want to let you know that you can relax and stop worrying about your parents. I saw your father this morning. He was on his way out of your apartment. I just happened to be checking to see if my milk had been delivered and so I stopped him. He said they had a very nice time down the shore. I didn't say anything about your call last night."

Eve interrupted. "Was he going down to the furniture store? I've got to call him right away."

"Oh no, Eve. He said he had to go back out of town on business. And he said your mother was on her way to Chicago to visit relatives."

There was silence on the other end of the line.

"Eve? Are you there?"

"Yes, Edna May. I'm sorry. I have to go. Thanks for the call. We'll be in touch soon." She hung up.

Eve repeated their conversation to Gordon, who said "Well, it doesn't clear anything up, but at least we know where they are now. Why do you still look so worried?"

Eve somberly replied. "We don't have any relatives in Chicago."

46

Walter Slezak's black Roadster barreled along a dirt road, kicking up huge clouds of dust in its wake. He had almost reached his destination in a secluded area of Hopewell, just outside of Princeton. Slezak pulled the automobile to a stop at what appeared to be a deep section of woods. But, nearly invisible to the rare passerby, another narrow dirt road led through the trees to an expansive open field. Two steel poles on either side of the road held a wrought iron sign over the entrance. "The German-American Bund" was cut out in ornate Gothic lettering.

The road continued to a main building, a quarter-mile straight ahead. To the left were a series of four identical barracks, each a single level, all long and narrow with an overhang and a short porch. To the right was a huge field, what looked to be a converted cornfield. Rubber tires were lined up flat, ten in a row. A twenty-foot wall stood alone with a coarse heavy rope hanging from the top. Dozens of men and teenage boys dotted the area. All were dressed in light brown button-down dress shirts, their collars tight to their necks. Their pants were dark brown with matching boots. Without exception, their heads sported short-cropped hair, pasted to their skulls.

Slezak was worried. He had not yet heard from Peter Lorre. Lorre had never failed him before. Slezak treated the little man's zeal for violence and his cold professionalism as a combination that had no possibility of failure. He retained the hope that Lorre's delay in returning was due only to his determination to complete both tasks with a high degree of perfection. As Slezak gazed across the fields at the uniformed Bund members methodically marching through the obstacle course singing the German National Anthem in unison, his momentary doubts were dispelled.

He got out of his car and headed into the main building. The plans must proceed on schedule, he thought. He passed through an empty foyer, decorated only by an Iron Cross hanging on one yellowed wall. He entered his office and made sure the door was closed securely behind him. He approached a mammoth oak desk in the middle of the room. He sat down on the swivel chair behind it and opened the top drawer on the right side. His hand reached far back into the well and grabbed onto a porcelain knob hidden on the farthest corner. He made a quarter turn of the knob and heard two clicks as a catch released from somewhere within the top of the desk. There was an unexpected banging on the front door and the muffled sound of someone yelling, "Hello? Anyone home?" Slezak quickly reached in and turned the knob back to its original position, the top of the desk again clicking as something locked in place.

Slezak left his office and went to the front door, where he found a middle-aged man peering in with his face pressed against the glass pane on the door. He opened the door, catching the man by surprise. "Can I help you?" he demanded.

"A-hem. Why, yes," the man began, attempting to conceal his embarrassment. "I had an appointment for an interview today. Frank Morgan's the name. I'm from the Trentonian newspaper."

Quite unusual for Slezak, he had completely forgotten about his other efforts to get good press for the Bund. "Why, yes. Of course. Mr. uh, uh…"

"Morgan."

"Morgan. Yes. Mr. Morgan. Do please come in." He led the reporter into his office. "I am so very happy that you are interested in our organization. I'll do whatever I can to help you with your story."

"A-hem. Well, thank you very much." Morgan took out his pad. "If you could just give me an overview first it would be a great start." He again indulged in his habit of nervously clearing his throat.

Slezak sized up the reporter and determined that he could be molded into any position Slezak desired – unlike the reporter from The Topic – and so he committed himself to making an impression that would be most favorable to the Bund. He offered a glass of beer and a plate of food to the hungry reporter as he reflected on the plight of the German people after the Great War and the isolation of Americans of German descent. Morgan furiously jotted notes in shorthand with his right hand while grabbing slices of limburger cheese and chunks of bratwurst with his left.

Slezak then led a tour of the spotless barracks as well as a demonstration of the agility and precision of the uniformed young men and boys. Slezak pointed out to Morgan that despite the nefarious claims of some fear mongers in the community, his group was solely dedicated to instilling responsibility and an uncompromising work ethic in the young adults who had been sent there by their parents.

Morgan left the grounds with a napkin full of bratwurst and a complimentary bottle of good German beer, thanking the kind Mr. Slezak and commenting, "Why, I had no idea that such a fine organization existed right here in our own backyard."

As he drove off, Slezak contentedly returned to his office and once again locked the door.

47

Eve was taking her turn behind the wheel, a situation Gordon thought was more dangerous than being shot at. He knew she was exhausted so he took it upon himself to keep her awake with what he thought was witty banter. "You know, if you end up putting only one dent into this car while you're driving, I believe Mr. Meek will think he got away lucky."

"And just what is that supposed to mean?" she snapped back.

"Well, you've been driving your dad's Hudson for, what, about three weeks and so far you've dented the front bumper, scratched the door when you side-swiped the milk truck, and shattered a tail light when you backed into that fence post last week."

Eve was not about to tell Gordon that there was now a fourth dent she had put in the car when she was trying to escape from the murderer at the Menjou's house. She simply ignored him and tightened her grip on the steering wheel. Not counting the fainting spell, she had kept her composure throughout this ordeal without a trace of panic.

"I've stayed quite composed for all I've been through," she proudly stated.

"Cool as a cucumber," Gordon chimed in.

She loosened up her hold on the steering wheel and let her fingers dance, hitting imaginary keys on a piano, her fingertips making the smoothest tapping sound.

"Day In, Day Out," Gordon said, guessing the tune she was tapping. It was a game they regularly played while driving.

"Correct," she nodded.

"I will now use my well-known ability to see into the future to predict your next selection." He held his fingers across his brow as if in deep meditation. "Our Love is Here to Stay."

Eve knew, of course, that it was now in her power to either prove him a charlatan at his so-called scientific crystal ball gazing, or confirm his supernatural powers.

"A-ha!" he proclaimed victory as she hit the first notes on the steering wheel.

"So…what's a dord?" she asked, changing the subject.

"You do not really want to know that."

"I do."

"You don't."

"Okay, but you'll be sorry."

"Oh, come on. Even Mitchell had no clue."

"When does he have a clue?"

"DORD??"

"Dord is a word that's not really a word." Gordon stopped as if he had explained the complete meaning in perfect detail.

"Oh, please," she mockingly pleaded, "do go on."

"It's a mistake. It's a mistake that it's a word."

"You know, Gordon, you would have thought that the lack of food and sleep would have made me dizzy. But, no… it took you defining a four letter word to do the job. I'm lost."

"I'm sorry. It takes some history to make it clear. You see, someone working on Webster's Dictionary put a notation when they were working on the pages marked 'D' – like capital 'D' – then 'o-r' - the word 'or' – and then small letter 'd.' It was an editing notation for someone to pick between those two: upper or lower case 'd'. A few more errors in the progression toward the final edit - like when a circle of people whisper something, one person to the next and the message has changed by the time it gets back to the first person – and, in the end, no one caught the error and dord became an official word in the English language according to Webster's Dictionary."

"My gosh!" Eve exclaimed, bursting with excitement. "That is earth shattering! We better pull over to the side of the road so you can write that story. I'm sure Mitchell will put in on the front page."

"Go ahead. Laugh." He waved her sarcasm aside. "They laughed at Edison, Marconi, Darwin, uh… who else did they laugh at?"

"The Three Stooges, The Marx Brothers, Laurel and Hardy…."

"Very funny. The part I just told you about is the history in a nutshell, but my point in writing about it is a more general observation, if we step back and look at the big picture. What dord is is a mistake. It's something that is there that shouldn't be there. And why is it there? Why is it included with all the real words like love, intelligence, humanity, spaghetti? It's because the gatekeepers, the authorities, society accepted something that should not be there.

"In the dictionary world it happened because the levels of communication were imperfect. They're human and that's okay. It's just a word. But, apply that to our world in general, that's my point. The German-American Bund is a dord – a big mistake. It's accepted by society as a legitimate organization, but that's wrong. You should see my story about them. It's hate mongering, pure and simple. There's an underlying threat of violence, a movement to create division by using the priority of pride in race. Sure, there are a lot of good German-Americans who support the Bund, but that's because they're unaware of what it really stands for. The Bund has escaped the scrutiny of the press, whose editors should say no, we won't allow good press to groups that preach hate. I'm sure that if the truth was told, then most German immigrants and other good people would reject them. But that's what it'll take – some good editing." Gordon realized that he was halfway standing up in the passenger side of the car. "Sorry about that."

"Don't apologize. Sounds like I've got a Pulitzer prize-winning boyfriend."

It was quiet in the car for the rest of the trip. They were getting close to their destination and the nervous anticipation of the last hour now settled into genuine anxiety. The hotel employee who had heard Karl Krell mention Plainsboro had set them on their next journey. That was where Karl Krell's used furniture warehouse was located. And the one thing they hoped to find in the two-story brick structure, more than anything, was answers.

48

In the mid-afternoon sun, a nine year old girl led a blind man up the incline of Washington Road and then down toward Lake Carnegie. Margaret O'Brien's tightly braided pigtails were the secular version of angel's wings. Her tiny left hand fit snugly into the gentle grip of Rhys Williams' right hand. Rhys had been without sight since a bout with measles almost took his life as a youngster. He was beloved by everyone in Princeton for his genuine exuberance, even while performing the mundane task of selling big cubes of ice. "The Iceman is anything but a cold man," the saying went.

But, it wasn't until one of the local girls from the orphanage took him under her wing that his happiness became complete. Almost every day after Rhys had finished working, the two of them would stroll down Nassau Street, cross the university campus, and then make the long trek to feed the birds and squirrels by the lake. Rhys kept a brown paper bag filled with roasted peanuts in his coat pocket. When they reached the grassy opening that led down to the water they'd follow the water line, stopping when Margaret saw a squirrel in the nearby woods or when Rhys would hear a duck flapping in the water.

They fed all the squirrels they could, but there was one that was Margaret's favorite. It was a small black squirrel, tinier than the others. It would come and eat right out of either of their hands. Margaret was particularly excited this day because she had just received a dime for her allowance and she was planning on treating Rhys to an ice cream soda.

"We can get two straws – one for you and one for me. And what kind of ice cream soda shall we get?" she asked, licking her lips at the thought of the upcoming treat.

"I think you should pick, Margaret. I like every kind of ice cream soda and whichever one you pick, that will be my favorite," Rhys replied in his lyrical Welsh accent.

Margaret decided to kid around with Rhys. "Okay. I know. I want a Dirt Soup ice cream soda."

"Mmm-mmmm. Sounds yummy to me."

They both laughed really silly laughs. But then Margaret's stopped short. Her hand dropped away from Rhys.

"What's wrong, darlin'. Tell me. What's the matter?"

"Oh no, Rhys. There's a man laying here in these leaves. I think he's dead."

49

The bell jingled on the door at the Topic. Lionel Atwill, the undertaker from Princeton Funeral and Memorial Company, Ltd. walked over to Spring Byington. She was busy typing and did not look up. Proving that she could do two things at once, she kept typing while asking, "May I help you?"

"I'm here on a confidential matter that I need to discuss with Mr. Mitchell," he replied in his distinct monotone.

"Oh, Mr. Atwill," Spring said, stopping her typing and looking up. Atwill always looked intensely serious but now even more so since he was wearing eyeglasses with thick black rims and even thicker lenses. His eyes made Miss Byington squirm in her seat. "I'll let Mr. Mitchell know you're here." She rushed past him into the publisher's office.

"Can we speak privately?" Atwill asked as Mitchell showed him into his office, closing the door behind him.

"Well, Lionel, what can I do for you?" Mitchell stated. "Anything wrong? Did we misspell your name in the late edition?"

"Grant, we've known each other for years. I feel quite uncomfortable being put in this position, but I feel I need to be frank." He stopped for emphasis and his eyes, not seeming to blink at all behind those magnified lenses, had Mitchell shift positions in his chair.

"Uh, sure, Lionel. Say what's on your mind. You know I'll do whatever I can."

"It's come to my attention that your sports writer," he emphasized the word sports, "has written a quite inflammatory article about the local German-American club," he paused again, his piercing stare causing Mitchell to look away. "You must admit that we have a very nice quiet community here in Princeton. Everyone gets along with one another. Now, Walter Slezak is a prominent member of that club, as are a number of other businessmen in the community. To publish a pack of lies that would besmirch the reputation of good people, well, that could be called yellow journalism, couldn't it?"

"I, uh, really didn't know you were a member of that organization, Lionel." Mitchell was unprepared for this attack.

"I am not a member of that group, Grant. I'm not a German, but that is not the point. Walter Slezak stopped over to see me and he was very upset. He has spent five years in this community building up a reputation, selling only the finest meats, I would add. Now he did not ask me to come here. He was just worried and needed to speak to someone. I could tell from his demeanor that he was not simply concerned about himself or his family – you do know he has a wife and seven children, plus a mother-in-law that lives with them? No, I could tell he was deeply concerned about our community and what it would be reduced to if this sort of muckraking spread."

"Now, Lionel. I hadn't even considered that…"

"Not considered, man!" Atwill's monotone rose up in volume, "how could you not consider the effect of such a story on a man's business?"

"Don't get upset, Lionel. I will personally make sure that before the story goes to print…."

"Goes to print?" Atwill interrupted, "After all I've said, you still plan on printing that garbage?"

"You haven't even seen the story. It will…."

"I don't need to see the story." Atwill stood up, his double-sized eyes enraged. "I'll just say this. If that story appears in your newspaper, I will withdraw all advertising from your paper permanently. As I'm sure you can surmise, Mr. Slezak will, as well. And I will be speaking with all of the merchants I can and I can assure you, The Topic won't be able to give away advertising space!" Lionel Atwill knew Grant Mitchell and how much the newspaper meant to him. A loss of revenue would be tantamount to the sun exploding. As he waited for Mitchell's reaction, all he saw was a determined adversary. And he smelled smoke. Cigar smoke.

He wasn't smoking. Mitchell wasn't smoking. Atwill wheeled around to see a bulky white-haired bespectacled man in a three-piece navy blue suit sitting on a high-backed chair in the corner. Atwill had come straight in, determined to berate Mitchell and had never even seen the stranger sitting silently in the corner.

Charles Coburn stood up. He was much older than Atwill and he was taller, stockier and very sure of himself. He strode over until he was toe to toe with the undertaker. He removed the cigar from his mouth and blew a puff of smoke right in Atwill's face. For the first time, Atwill blinked.

"Mr. Attaboy," Coburn began, without the undertaker

even entertaining the notion of correcting the mispronunciation, "I'd like to introduce myself. My name is Coburn. Charles Coburn. Mr. Coburn to you. I am the new silent, or should I say not-so-silent partner in The Princeton Topic." Coburn paced back and forth in front of the shell-shocked Atwill. "I have decided to expand beyond my import-export empire on the West Coast and, let's say, diversify. I've always had a passion for real journalism, professional stuff – not that namby-pamby nonsense you see all across the country. That's why I'm backing Mitchell here. Putting the full financial capabilities of my resources at his disposal." He stopped pacing and stared directly into Atwill's face. "And let me tell you," he poked his right index finger into Atwill's chest in perfect timing with his cadence, "we're not going to be pushed around or blackmailed or told what to print or what not to print by you or anyone else. Now get out of here and take your business with you! Being the only paper in town, you'll find your opportunities limited. I'll discuss with my partner the possibility that we might, in good time, agree to accept advertising from you again." He paused and then added, "At double the rate, my good man. Now… GO!"

Atwill fumbled with the door before rushing off in fear and confusion. The two men enclosed in the office burst out in great belly laughs that simply could not be contained.

"Didn't I tell you that you should be glad to see me, Grant?" Coburn chided.

"All right, all right," Mitchell conceded, "but I really never knew I had a brother-in-law with such creative storytelling talents."

Coburn walked over with outstretched hands and upturned palms and said, "Well, Grant, did I earn that fifty bucks I wanted to borrow?"

50

Guy Kibbee burped. Aline and Shirley, playing checkers on the floor, both giggled.

"S'not funny," Guy moaned, rubbing his belly. He wound and wound another big string of linguine on his fork and stuffed it in his mouth. He didn't know if it was his erratic eating pattern or all the peanuts he'd been munching on – boy, he loved peanuts – but he had the worst case of indigestion. "Think I need some bicarbonate of soda, dear."

"Well, when you take that old mattress down to the trash bins, you can pick some up at the store. You've just plumb used up all we had," his wife said.

He burped again and pushed the plate away from him. He got up and went over to his two girls. He studied the board for a moment and then moved one of Aline's red checkers and nudged Shirley to make the next move. She grinned and then tap, tap, tap – triple jumped Aline's pieces.

"I win," Shirley gleefully announced.

"Not fair," Shirley's mom complained.

Guy smiled and flopped the mattress over his shoulder and headed out the door. He had to stop at the first set of steps while the elderly couple that lived next to him hobbled up the stairs. The gentleman had started walking with a cane and each step was an effort. Guy waited patiently until they passed. He continued down, only slightly annoyed that they hadn't even thanked him for his courtesy. As he entered the stairwell to the second floor, he crashed right into Allen Jenkins, who was heading in the same direction.

"Sorry," they both said.

Jenkins was sweating profusely and Guy thought the man might be sick. "You all right, Jenkins?" Kibbee asked.

"Sure. Just in a hurry. Sorry again," Jenkins mumbled as he rushed ahead of him down the steps.

This last encounter was observed by a set of eyes peeking out through the slightly parted door of Edna May Oliver's apartment. But it was not Edna May Oliver.

Inside her room, with an aching back from standing perched at the doorway, was Sergeant James Gleason. For the past two hours he had replayed the conversation over in his head a thousand times and he could still not fathom how he had let Edna May bamboozle him into staking out the suspicious movements inside 26 Witherspoon Street. She had detailed with precision the many unexplainable events in the hallway and rooms of the five story building. So, with an unidentified dead body discovered almost right out the back door of the building, he decided that he could not afford to ignore her suggestion.

When he saw the silhouette of a heavy object, maybe a dead body, being carried down the hall Gleason decided to act. He sprung out of the doorway, or as much like a spring as he could manage at his age and with an aching back. "Hold it right there, mister," he demanded.

Kibbee's full figure appeared in the hall, revealing the mattress lumped over his back.

"Sure. Sure. What's up, Sergeant?"

Clearly embarrassed, Gleason pointed to the mattress. "Just wanted to know if you, uh, wanted some help lugging that thing down the steps."

"Well, thanks for the offer. That's most kind of you, but, no – I'm fine." He trudged on past, leaving Gleason to sulk back into the apartment.

That's it, he thought. Two hours is enough. She won't be able to say I didn't try. Just then the door burst open. It was Officer Pendleton.

"Another dead body, Chief. Down by the lake."

51

Gleason and Pendleton arrived at the lake to find the coroner, Eric Blore, already there.

"Been here long, Blore?" Gleason greeted the man.

Blore put his two hands in the air. "I just got here. I haven't even removed my mittens yet."

"Sorry I asked."

"I was in the middle of my afternoon tea, Sergeant. I am not very happy." He removed his mittens and examined the body.

"Well," said Gleason, peering over Blore's shoulder, "it wasn't my fault you had to come here."

"If you could catch the killer then maybe I WILL get to have my tea."

"Wait a second. Are you trying to say this is connected to the Menjou murder?"

"Sergeant," Blore said as if talking to Pendleton, "there has not been a murder in Princeton in over six years and now, suddenly, three in less than two days. Pure coincidence? I think not."

"Good point, Bl…."

"Oh my gosh," Blore groaned. "It's that butcher fellow."

"Was he a friend of yours?" Pendleton asked.

"No. No. No," Blore said. "I mean, oh my gosh, he's disgusting. This little man gave me the heebie-jeebies when he was alive. Look. He still has that evil grin on his face now he's dead."

"Geez. I see what you mean," Pendleton agreed, peering in at the dead man's face.

Blore stood up and buttoned his coat. "I'll know more after the autopsy. This one I'll do with my eyes closed. Anyway, for now I can safely say: single gunshot wound, very close range. And, the victim had recently fired a gun himself and was preparing to shoot again."

"What makes you say that?" Gleason asked.

"The gun was still in his hand, cocked and ready to fire – one bullet missing, and powder burns on his fingers." Blore put his mittens back on. "This weather is too cold for murder. Gentlemen, goodbye." He turned and left them standing at the lake.

"Pendleton, this stiff worked for Walter Slezak, the guy Miss Oliver claims threatened Gordon Radits." Gleason turned to leave. "I think it's time we had a talk with Mr. Slezak."

52

"How was that rib eye steak, Sergeant?" Walter Slezak looked up from packing a slab of ribs to greet Sergeant Gleason.

"I wouldn't know, Mr. Slezak," he snapped, "with all the murders going on around town, I haven't had time to sleep, let alone eat."

"Oh, I'm so sorry to hear that. I hope your schedule soon returns to normal," he attempted to placate the irritated policeman.

"Can I speak with you privately, sir?" Gleason asked.

Slezak led him into the back room, while Pendleton stayed near the door, keeping an eye on the top round roast.

"Tell you why I'm here," Gleason got right to the point, "your employee, Peter Lorre, has been found dead."

This was news to Slezak. He knew something had gone awry since his accomplice had not returned, but this turn of events was unexpected and it took all of his skill not to react in a way that would arouse suspicion.

"This is horrible, Sergeant. My God. How did it happen? Was it an accident?" Slezak paced nervously.

"He was murdered, Slezak. Shot and killed."

This news was almost more shocking. Did Radits shoot Lorre? Slezak couldn't believe that Radits had or even knew how to use a gun. If not Radits, then who? His thoughts kept him silent and prompted Gleason to comment, "You're awful quiet. Is there anybody in particular you suspect of the shooting?"

"Sergeant, this man simply worked in the butcher shop for me. We were not friends, not close. He was just a worker." He continued, trying to distance himself from Lorre, "Why, his performance was not even exceptional enough for me to take notice. I would not even say that he would be missed, but at the same time, it is a very sad and tragic event."

"Yeah, yeah." Gleason brushed aside the hollow words. "But I've got some other information that makes this whole story look like some funny business is going on."

"I don't understand, Sergeant."

"I've got some reliable sources who tell me that you recently threatened Gordon Radits." Gleason looked Slezak squarely in the eye. "And you had Lorre standing right next to him with a gun pointed at his head. What do you have to say about that?"

"Why, that's nonsense, Sergeant. Sheer nonsense." Slezak prided himself on keeping calm in even the most stressful situations. "It's true that I have been calling The Topic trying to provide Radits with a story concerning an upcoming football game. No more. No less. I have been unsuccessful in communicating that information to the young man, but a threat? What would I want to threaten him about?"

"C'mon, Mr. Slezak. Isn't it true that you're connected with the German-American Bund Club?"

"Why yes, certainly. But what would that have to do with it?"

"Gordon Radits was writing a story about your group. A quite critical piece, from what I gather."

"Sergeant," Slezak was masterfully maintaining his composure, "I had no idea that this story was being written. How could I know? I do not get the inside scoops, as they say, on what The Topic plans to print. Furthermore, I thought you were looking for this reporter. Isn't he wanted as an accessory to murder or something?"

"He's wanted for questioning," Gleason admitted, "but that has nothing to do with Lorre's murder."

"Now that you mention it, maybe it could, Sergeant. You see, I can account for everywhere I've been the last twenty-four hours, whether it's been here at work or home with my family or with my club. But I ask you this, does this Radits fellow have an alibi? If he's already involved in the murder of Professor Menjou, then wouldn't it be natural to ask him exactly where he was when another murder took place the next day?"

"Mr. Slezak, you let the police worry about who's a suspect and who's not. I'm just warning you. I don't like people threatening other people. Don't let it happen again.

And by the way, your liver is on the floor."

Slezak, without even realizing it, had knocked some pieces of meat off one of the prep tables. As he picked them up and put them back on the table, Gleason started to leave. "Better not let the health department see that. I gotta' go, but I'll be in touch. Don't go anywhere." Gleason motioned to Pendleton and they left for the police station.

53

Gordon and Eve had been sitting in the parked car for over an hour. When they had first pulled up to the Krell Furniture Warehouse, Eve had been surprised by the changes. There was a high chain link fence all around the perimeter of the property. Tall bushy evergreens, some eight to ten feet and others nearly fully grown, had been planted to augment the privacy of the fence.

"What's the big secret about used furniture?" Gordon asked.

"This is all new to me," Eve replied.

Right after an unknown car had entered the grounds, Eve and Gordon decided to approach the main gate that was being closed by two men in typical work clothes. They didn't move, however, when they noticed the guns strapped to holsters around the men's chests.

Eve suggested they drive right to the nearest telephone and call the police, but that plan evaporated a second later when a door to the car opened and her father got out. He gave a nod of approval to one of the men at the gate and then turned and entered the building.

"That's it. We need to know what this is all about,"

she started up the car and drove right to the gate.

The two men blocked their entrance and came over to the car. "Sorry, ma'am. This warehouse is not open to the public. You can try the store downtown."

"I'm here to see my father, Karl Krell," she demanded.

Unprepared for such a visit, one of them retreated from the gate and entered the side door of the warehouse. The other kept his foot on the running board, as if to prevent the car from moving. Minutes later, the guard came out and waved to let them through. He led them into a cold, unheated structure. The huge storage space was stacked with beds, dressers and tables. Directly inside an industrial-sized garage door was a truck with a giant black tarp covering the cargo area. Sitting next to the truck on wooden pallets were long rectangular bins filled with apples.

They were led up a set of metal stairs toward a loft space with an enclosed office. An elderly man emerged from the office, followed by a teary-eyed woman with a brown kerchief over her head. She was tugging a young boy with a grimy face behind her. They swiftly brushed by Eve and Gordon with their heads turned away. The door to the office opened and Eve gasped, "Dad!" They rushed into a tight embrace. "I've been so worried. I didn't know what happened to you." All her emotions flared in one rumbling cry.

"It will all work out, Eve. It will all be okay." Karl Krell comforted his daughter and slowly she seemed to regain her composure. But then she bolted back out of his arms.

"Where's mom? Is she okay? What's this about Chicago? We don't even know a single person in Chicago!"

Gordon thought it interesting that she hadn't even got to mentioning that she was wanted for murder.

Karl bit his lip, trying to decide how to proceed. "She's

fine," he said in an even tone. He looked over at an industrial wall clock with large numbers on it, nailed behind the desk. "We have some time before I must depart. I cannot go into great detail, but I think it is best if I explain what I can to you. Sit down," and looking toward Gordon, "you too, my boy."

54

Karl pulled up a chair in front of them. He put his hand on Eve's arm. "First, let me assure you, your mother is absolutely safe. She is not in harm's way. But, in order for you to understand the current situation, I must preface it with some history." He paused, staring into the air, as if gathering strength.

"Your mother and I have not discussed our backgrounds much with you. We were both born in Russia, that much we have told you. But the details, that we have left vague. There are many immigrants in America – all countries, races, and ethnicities seem to have found their way here. But, not all are accepted equally. For someone like your mother and I, the less details we talked about, the better chances we had of making a life for ourselves…and for you. But, there have been a few times when events made our blending in not so important.

"My family was originally from the Russian town of Kishinev, a typical small farm town not too far from Odessa – which was near the Black Sea. My father and mother had a small farm where they raised chickens and some crops, like potatoes and beans. We were poor and we struggled, but we all worked hard together and there was always food on the table and we had enough clothes to keep us warm in the winter.

"Things got tougher for us and most Russians during the economic crisis in the 1890's. Governments are always apt to find scapegoats for the plight of their people and the anti-Semitism that had already existed in our country became even more inflamed. The result was pogroms - organized attacks on Jewish families all over Russia. People who had been our good friends either ignored us or spat at us. I was much too young to fully understand the pure hatred and violence that was descending upon us.

"One night, it was after midnight and the moon was the only light for as far as the eye could see. I was laying in bed near a window when I heard frantic movements in the other room. The door burst open and it was my mother, she was weeping uncontrollably. 'Get up! Get up quickly!' she cried and since I had not yet fallen off to sleep, I bounced out of my bed, my heart racing. My body was yanked this way and that as she hurriedly placed one sweater after another over my head. She grabbed a burlap sack that she had thrown on the floor when she entered the room. She pushed it into my arms, gained enough composure to speak and said, 'Karl. There are mobs coming. They are angry. They do not see what they are doing, and they have murdered' she stopped, choking back the tears, 'the Grehevs, the Mellinsk families. They are all gone. Just tonight.' I said to my mother, 'We won't let them do that to us, Mother. We'll fight.' 'No, no, listen,' she told me, 'there are too many to fight right now. Father has figured out what to do and we must listen. There is no time for anything else. Now you take this sack and go out to the back of the barn. You will see your father there and he will tell you what to do.'

"She gave me such a hug I can still feel it. 'Now, go,' she said and shoved me off. When I went out, the moon was no longer the only light. I could see, in the distance, three distinct areas where flames were shooting up into the sky. The smell of wood burning seeped into my throat. I ran as fast as I could, the sack in my right hand bobbing up and down. When I reached the clearing behind the barn, there was my father, sweat dripping off his face, digging furiously with a heavy shovel. When he saw me, he stopped only long enough to hand me a second shovel and point to the hole. 'Dig' he ordered. As we dug this rectangular hole deeper and deeper, my father started looking away nervously toward the town. Finally, he dropped the shovel and grabbed me by the shoulders, squeezing with his hands like a vise grip. 'Listen' he told me, 'the mobs are coming and they will kill us if they have their way. Now do as you are told. We have no time to argue.' He tossed a blanket into the hole. 'You get down there and lay down on that blanket. I am going to cover you with another blanket and then I am going to cover you with dirt.' He handed me a piece of wood that he had long ago whittled to act as a straw. The center had been dug out to allow for air flow. 'You will use this to get air from the surface. After I cover you with dirt, I am putting hay over top. They will not find you. I will make sure they will not find you. I promise you.' I cried, and asked my father, 'But what about you and mother?' He replied, 'Do as I say. We will be all right. I have a different hiding place for us. Now go!' And without a further pause for emotion, he pushed me into the small pit and started shoveling dirt on me. The dirt was already on my clothes when I got down on the blanket. The ground was so cold I shivered through the blanket. I pulled the top blanket over me to hide the smell of the dirt, but it was useless. Within seconds I could hear him patting the ground down, scraping the dirt around the wooden straw to make sure it wasn't visible. Then like light rain on a spring day, I heard scattered clouds of hay being piled on top of the earth.

"For awhile, all I could hear was my own heavy breathing echoing in my confined space. Then the sound of footsteps, horses and angry voices. There were so many angry voices that the words spilled over each other, but some would sift through to stand out like a dagger to my heart. It was when the voices were the loudest that I realized they had set the pile of hay above me on fire. This must mean the house, the barn, they were all gone. I lay buried there for so long I don't even know. Eventually, I started scratching at the dirt with my fingernails.

"When I broke through to the surface, the dirt covering my face mixed with my tears to become a salty mud dripping off my chin. Everything had been destroyed, burnt to the ground. And my parents, murdered.

"My anger could have consumed the whole town of Kishinev, the whole country of Russia, but, luckily, a friend of mine whose family had just endured the same agony found me rummaging through the remains of my home. His name was Adolph Menjou, and his anger had been tempered by a mind that thought differently than mine. Ever since I met him at the age of five he was consumed with the joy of music. I do not know whether it was the music that made him look at the world differently, or that his view of the world made music possible. Adolph reasoned that since the government was instigating the hatred and the mobs were too big and too strong, we could count on no one in Russia to help us to avenge these atrocities. And so, we made plans to leave Russia. To get away, but to never forget what had happened.

"We made our way south to the outskirts of Odessa, where we were able to join with a small group of others who had similar tales. We moved eastward along the Black

Sea toward Simferopol. Eventually, after weeks of travelling, we were smuggled aboard a cargo ship. Our final destination was America, but we had plenty of time to dream and to remember. Adolph and I made a pact that we would come back for those left behind, and the others in our group were anxious to be included. It took many years in America before we had the resources to go back. But we did. More than once. We smuggled hundreds of people out of Russia before they could be murdered.

"Your mother is one of the refugees that we brought back, as well as her cousin, who you know as Abigail Menjou."

Here, Eve was forced to cut in. "Mrs. Menjou is mom's cousin? You mean I'm related to her?"

"Yes," her father replied.

"That woman accused me of murdering the Professor! Oh, wait. I'm sorry. You don't know about any of this. I'm so sorry, dad, but Professor Menjou has been killed."

Karl's face was incredibly sad and somber. "I do know about that, and it does make me grieve to have lost such a dear friend. But let me finish and then I will explain.

"We continued our missions for some time, operating in total secrecy and with a select group whose loyalty was unquestionable. But, somehow, a newspaper discovered the story and splashed it all over their front page. A philanthropic organization offered us medals of honor and promises of support, but the secrecy had been compromised. We were no longer able to smuggle a pack of cigars past a reporter, let alone smuggle people out of a country. So, we had to be content with the knowledge that we had accomplished some good, saved many lives. And, we moved on.

"Regrettably, the events in Germany over the last few

years began to attract my attention. As news escalated to the point where I could see little difference between the pogroms in Russia and what was going on in Germany, I became very concerned. I felt that this time it could be even more far-reaching than what I went through. Something I never thought possible. But I had become settled and kept resisting the temptation to even mention it to anyone.

"Then, we heard of the events of June 4th of this year. The SS St. Louis was carrying 963 refugees trying to flee from Germany. They had been denied their attempts to disembark in Cuba, and then they were turned away when the boat docked in Florida. The reports said they had to stay on the ship and return to Germany. My anger seethed and I could sit still no longer. With your mother's blessing, I met with the Menjous and they did not hesitate for a moment. That very night, we decided that we must act. The only other member of our original group that was still alive was Alan Mowbray. It took days for us to track him down as he had moved a number of times. When we found him living in New York City, he was eager to join our cause. He became the Menjou's butler, as a cover to work closely with us.

"Working surreptitiously, we engaged the services of some rum runners who had lost much of their income when prohibition was repealed. We were able to save some of the refugees being returned on the SS St. Louis. As disgusting as it sounds, we replaced them with cadavers and floated the rumor of an epidemic of a new strain of flu on board." Karl looked at the clock. "I must go shortly, but this was much of the history that is necessary for you to understand the events of the last day or two. I will try and clear this in your minds before I leave. You see, somehow, someone found out about our current rescue service. When we decided to go beyond the people on the boat, to organize for the long struggle to bring people out of Germany, we knew we would be in a more dangerous position than before. This may be hard to imagine, but those in charge in Germany – and their sympathizers here – are far more aggressive in their hatred than the Russians were. I foresee events worsening, and a small effort did not seem enough to save many of those whose lives are at risk.

"Your mother and I have been telling you we were going to the beach each week end, but we have been instead driving to Philadelphia as part of the chain that brings people into the country. Though what we are doing is illegal, we look to the Statue of Liberty – the Mother of Exiles – as our validation. After being smuggled aboard the ships, refugees are placed in hidden compartments in a cargo truck and brought here to rest a bit. Then they are dispersed to a network of volunteers across the country. When we got news of the breach in security, we called Adolph - Professor Menjou - from Philadelphia. Unfortunately, it was too late for him to act and we lost a great friend. Since you were at the scene of the murder, we did not know how much danger you were in. The assassin might have thought you saw him. Add in the fact that you are my daughter – those connections put your life at risk. We could not go to the police with this information, since what we are doing is outside the law.

"So, we came to the conclusion that you would have to be arrested for the murder. In jail, we hoped, at least you would be safe. Of course, never in my right mind would I have contemplated that my well-behaved daughter would get in cahoots with this young whippersnapper and, as they say in the picture shows, take it on the lam from the police." He turned to Gordon. "I hope you know that

I'm holding you responsible for her safety, young man."

"Just the way I want it, sir," Gordon replied.

"And I hold you responsible for mom," Eve poked a finger at her dad.

"Exactly so, and that is why she is not here," he answered. "Let's just let it go for now that she is safe, secure and you will get to see her as soon as we get the all clear. Now we do have to go."

"Wait," Eve said. "What about Mrs. Menjou, or Aunt Abigail or whatever I should call her? She's alone in that house where the Professor was already murdered."

"Keep calm, Eve. Mr. Mowbray is with her and his first duty is to watch out for her safety."

"And what about the breach in security? Was it an informer?" Gordon tentatively asked, feeling awkward butting in to the father and daughter conversation.

"The informer," he began, "is somewhat of a mystery himself. You see, one night I received a call at the Blue Pearl Hotel asking for a Mr. Smith. I was hesitant to take the call since it was agreed that I would only be contacted there in the event of a dire emergency and there were no indications that such a thing had arisen. Nevertheless, I decided to answer. The man first confirmed that he was talking to Mr. Joseph Smith. He then said that he had very important information for me but that he would first state a series of facts to prove his legitimacy. He called me by my real name – something we had all agreed would never ever be done – and told me where I was going with the truck, what the contents of the truck were, and added for a last bit of convincing, the phrase 'SS St. Louis.' I demanded to know what he wanted, never acknowledging that anything he had just mentioned was true. He tried to reassure me that his intentions were honorable. He claimed that he had gone in with the wrong crowd and had just come to his senses. He had a lot of information to give me which he said was of the utmost urgency. He said he was calling because the lives of all involved were in immediate danger.

"We arranged to meet the next morning at the bus station on Perry Street in Trenton. I asked how I would recognize him and he said I would remember him. He once bought a used basinet with a red painted stripe on it for his new son. I apparently told him that it was the only one like it that I'd ever seen, and when he did not have the full payment for it I sold it to him for half the price. And he was right, I did remember him. He was a short stocky man with close cropped blonde hair."

"Yes," Eve said, "I remember him, too. I was helping with the cash register that day. What happened at the bus station?"

"I'm afraid he didn't show up," the words came from Gordon rather than Mr. Krell.

"How do you know that?" Eve asked as Karl looked on.

"Because he was killed in the alley behind your home yesterday."

55

Gordon suddenly used both hands and frantically rummaged through his pockets, his pants, his jacket. "Rats!" he yelled. "I was there. I actually fell over the body in the alley and I found a slip of paper in his pocket. I took it, but it looks like I lost it."

"Wait!" Eve cried, grabbing her pocketbook. "I found that paper on the floor when you ran out of the dungeon. I forgot to give it back to you." She had a small pocketbook but she had to empty it in order to find the little square of paper. Out tumbled a leather coin purse with a brass snap, two tubes of lipstick, a handful of assorted hair pins, safety pins, paper clips, one sharp and two broken pencils, receipts for packs of gum, shoelaces, a pocket mirror covered with scratches, some loose change that escaped from her coin purse, folded up advertisements for shoes, and finally the little brown piece of paper. "Here," she said unfolding it on the table, "seems very cryptic to me."

All three of them stared at the writing:

40°44'34.089"N73°50'43.842"W

"The World's Fair!" Gordon screamed, almost jumping out of his seat. "Remember when we went to New York for the World's Fair and we saw Roosevelt?" Gordon wondered why Eve seemed confused. "Oh, wait a minute. We went in, let's see, the middle of June and then I took you again for your birthday in July. That's right. You weren't there the first time I went. It was April 30th, the opening day of the World's Fair." The World's Fair was likely Gordon's favorite place on Earth. It consumed his passion for science and the amazing prospects for the future. He had made three trips already, including being one of the first in line on opening day.

"There is a capsule, a time capsule that they filled with representations of life on Earth, 1939. Everything from a Mickey Mouse watch to something by Professor Einstein. They had a ceremony and buried it on opening day, not to be opened until the year 6939." Gordon tapped his hand on the little piece of paper. "And this is the location where it is buried! But then," by now Gordon was pacing back and forth in front of the desk, "it must mean that this thing is a really big clue. If only we knew what that message was about, more details. What's it for? Or exactly when is something going to happen there?"

"Maybe," Eve suggested, "if we could look at the schedule of events at the fair, something might stick out."

"Yeah, great! Wait." Gordon stopped. "What day is it?" He rushed over to a calendar hanging on the wall. The calendar was a gift from Bailey's Grocery Store and had their name, address and phone number printed above the dates. "Oh my gosh! It's October 29th!" he yelled.

"What does that mean?" Karl asked.

"Tomorrow is the last day of the World's Fair for 1939. It closes for the season. If anything is planned, it's going to happen tomorrow."

56

The man lifted a spoon and scooped four portions of sugar into his tea cup. He stirred so vigorously that some of the liquid spilled over into the waiting saucer. He picked up the cup and took a sip, making a slurping noise that attracted the attention of the other diners.

"Miss Byington," Charles Coburn said, "I feel that as the brother-in-law of the publisher, I am a part of the Princeton Topic family."

"That's so nice," she smiled.

"Why, I've been in town for less than a day and I can feel the spirit of journalism swimming through my veins."

"Oh my," she added.

From his pocket, Coburn pulled out a half-smoked cigar, which he lit with great care. "It was most gracious of you to accept my invitation to dinner, Miss Byington."

"Oh, no, Mr. Coburn. It was so wonderful of you to ask."

Coburn took a puff on his cigar and then smiled in appreciation of the lady's compliment. "Thank you, Spring. May I call you Spring? You've been a devoted worker at The Topic for many years, from what Grant tells me. Years that don't show, I might add." He paused for a smile. "I'm sure that sometimes you must wonder about your future, I mean, you never know about the newspaper business. Sell out every edition one day – next day, gone," he snapped his fingers in the air, "out of business."

"Yes, sir. May I help you?" the waiter ran over to their table.

"I, uh, no thank you. Not right now."

"Okay. Sorry, sir," the waiter said, making some snapping motions with his fingers as he stormed off.

"As I was saying before I was interrupted," Coburn continued, "you should really start to seriously think about your future. You know, you can't stay as young as you are forever." As he rolled out the last sentence, he fumbled in his coat pocket for a folded brochure. It was a policy for the Acme Life Insurance Company, a fly-by-night broker that offered a fifty-fifty split with anyone who could sell a policy. In the training sessions for new agents, they highly recommended buying one way tickets out of town before trying to sell new policies.

"Charles," Spring sang, batting her eyelashes, "this is so sudden. I didn't realize you were the romantic type."

Some people get caught off guard in conversations more than others, but the one trait Charles was proud of was his ability to adapt to new circumstances. "Spring, those blue eyes of yours just had me under their spell from the first time I saw them."

"They're green. But thank you, Charles." Spring was ready to say more but spotted something out of the corner of her eye and rose quickly to leave the table. "Excuse me for just a moment, Charles."

Just seating himself at a corner table near the back door was Allen Jenkins. Jenkins was wearing a wrinkled navy blue suit that was obviously too big for him. He was nervous, removing his hat and sliding it back and forth between his hands on the table top. He knocked over the centerpiece, a tiny plastic vase with artificial flowers in it. He carefully righted it, but then knocked it over again. He was looking all around the dining room, twenty or so tables and booths, but he did not see the person he was looking for. Spring Byington marched all the way across the room until she stopped behind his table. Next to her was a tall coat rack that stood at least a foot taller than her, made of a thick sturdy wood to carry the weight of heavy winter coats. Spring grabbed the rack by the center pole and with a sudden burst of energy, brought the pole right down on the back of Allen Jenkins' head. The force of the blow threw his head down onto the hardwood table top, causing him to loudly groan in pain.

Spring Byington pulled the rack back up and magically transformed her glare into a sympathetic smile. "Oh, Mr. Jenkins. I am so, so sorry. I must have accidentally knocked over the coat stand. My apologies." She turned and walked back to her table while Jenkins mumbled, "Yeah, yeah. It's okay."

The cigar was now dangling off the edge of Charles Coburn's open mouth. He had been watching the whole scene unfold. He looked befuddled as she sat down.

"No questions, Mr. Coburn, please. It will all be explained in good time. Now, how about a nightcap?"

57

Bucky Carradine was perched on a three-legged stool peering through the small window in his attic room. A few men in overcoats crossed the street this way or that, creating geometric patterns in his mind. He looked at his watch, the illuminated hands ticking in a mechanical lock step that reminded him of his days in the war. He looked over at his night table where the receiver was sitting on its side against the base of the telephone. The long unending tone of the phone off its hook made him smile devilishly. He got up, stretched, then carefully placed the stool back under his kitchen table. He changed his shirt, removing one dark blue button down and replacing it with another exactly like it. He passed the mirror without even the slightest urge to look in it. He stopped at the crate full of Scotch on the floor and picked up the one bottle among them that had already been opened. He took it back across the room and sat down on his mattress. He raised a shot glass from his night table and filled it about a quarter full, tilted it just enough to wet his lips and his tongue, then deliberately wiped his mouth with the back of his shirt sleeve. He carefully poured the remainder of the Scotch back in the bottle and returned it to the crate.

It's time, he thought. He hurried his movements a bit now, putting on his overcoat and his big felt hat. He pushed down the brim to cover as much of his features in shadow as it possibly could and then quickly left his dark and lonely room.

There was not a soul in the stairway and every step he took made creaking sounds that echoed down the hallway. As he passed from one floor to the next he heard the sounds of a quiet conversation in a melodic foreign lilt, then the high-pitched static of a radio station already signed off for the night, then one still playing soft music. The second floor was completely silent, either because the Krells were not at home or because of the strict demand for quiet mandated by Miss Oliver. Or both, he thought.

He reached the street, looked both ways. It was empty. In his determination to reach his destination, he did not notice that the police car sitting directly across from the door from which he had just exited was occupied. Maybe he thought that Officer Pendleton was asleep – since that location was his favorite and the car was often parked there. But on this night, Pendleton's eyelids couldn't have been open any wider than if he'd had toothpicks propping them up. This night, he was under strict orders from Sergeant Gleason to down one cup of black coffee every fifteen minutes while on duty. He was now on his fifth hour of duty and he desperately needed to find a bathroom.

58

It was after midnight and Sergeant Gleason was still in his office, thinking. From time to time his feet would slip off the desk and it would jolt him awake. He would reposition and get back to thinking. That phone call from Karl Krell earlier in the evening had turned his whole case upside down.

While he never wholeheartedly believed that Eve could have murdered Professor Menjou, he had to follow procedure and, if she hadn't escaped, it might even have been an open and shut case. That is, with some pretty convincing testimony from Abigail Menjou. Of course, the first tiny speck of doubt that had crawled into his brain was when his repeated attempts to question the grieving widow were continuously delayed. True, she was in shock - as any wife would be at the sudden death of her husband. But after she had so clearly identified the murderer, it was just a little too suspicious that she kept having pressing matters or previous engagements that prevented her from talking to the police.

Karl Krell's phone call about the unidentified dead man had come from out of the blue. Gleason fought the urge to suspect that there might be some other funny business going on when Krell kept claiming secrecy, because after all, he was a respected member of the Princeton business community. So, when he said, "Listen, Sergeant, I am not at liberty to divulge everything because lives are at stake," Gleason was inclined to take him at his word. He sometimes had a hunch about people, and Krell was a good egg in his book.

That was the only reason Gleason had acted so quickly to call the New York City authorities. He felt a little out of his league calling New York to warn them about a threat to the World's Fair based on some numbers and letters on a piece of paper. But, he did it. If they laughed after he got off the phone, so what. He passed on the information in good faith.

The fact that Eve and Gordon were secure in Krell's office gave him some relief. His reputation would be mud if the known prime suspect and her boyfriend were seen window shopping on Nassau Street or at the local dance.

If only he'd hear from Edna May. She had promised an immediate call if she found anything – yet, not a word. His feet started to slip off the desk again and it reminded him of Pendleton staked out on Witherspoon Street. With the Krells all away, there's no point in him watching all night, or sleeping all night, as the case might be. A little snooze, Gleason thought and then I'll go over and tell him to call it a night.

59

Bucky had taken the car that was at his disposal from behind the butcher shop and had driven out of town. After driving around for awhile, it was close to two o'clock in the morning before he arrived at the Bund compound. He had to pass fully alert security patrols, even at this late hour. When he entered the office of the main building, Walter Slezak shouted, "You fool! Do you see what time it is?"

"I was waiting for your call, Mister Slezak."

"I did call," Slezak yelled. "I called and called and the telephone was always busy. Who were you talking to for so long? You knew to expect my call!"

"I wasn't talking to anyone."

"The line was busy."

"I guess I'll have to call for service. It must be broken. I was sitting right there by the phone all night. It never rang. Not once. Just sat there. Quieter than a mouse."

"All right. Shut up." Slezak was fuming.

Bucky looked around the room. He had expected other people to be there, but it was just he and Slezak.

"What are you looking for?" Slezak demanded.

"Nothing. I thought I heard a noise. Probably just going stir crazy from sitting in my room waiting for the telephone to ring."

Slezak put both hands down on the table. "This is very serious business, my friend. We are counting on you. Now pay attention." He slid his hand into the opened drawer of the desk, reached in and twisted the hidden porcelain knob. A large piece of the desktop popped open. Slezak lifted it and locked it in an upright position.

"This is your area," he pointed with a pencil to a spot on the heretofore hidden map.

"Are there other areas?" Bucky asked.

Slezak walked over and stuck his face not more than an inch from Bucky's. He sniffed. "You've been drinking. You slob. What did I tell you about that habit? That stuff can kill you and it's probably going to."

"Sorry, sir." Bucky slinked back away from the desk.

"So you are aware, this is your assigned area." Slezak allowed Bucky to study the map while he went over to a safe hidden behind a file cabinet. The sound of the tumblers clicking into place took just brief seconds. A creaking safe door opened and Slezak removed a small black leather bag.

"Oh, I get to be a doctor," Bucky joked, reacting to what looked like a physician's medical bag in Slezak's hands.

"It's much more than that, my friend."

He handed the bag to Bucky, who marveled at how heavy it was. Slezak again demanded his attention. "You can see on this map where you are to go in New York City. When you reach this point," he pointed to a big "X" marked on the map, "you are to open the bag with this key." He placed a small brass key into Bucky's palm. "Inside the bag will be a printed sheet. You are to follow the printed instructions word for word. You will have less than ten minutes to complete your task. At that point, you will follow the instructions on that page in order to make your escape. Do you understand?"

"Yes, I think so."

Slezak marched over to the corner of the room where there was a small coffee pot. He poured the liquid into a tin cup and handed it to Bucky. "It's old and most likely bitter, but you need to sober up. NOW!" Bucky gulped the whole cup down.

"I repeat," Slezak commanded, "do not open the bag until the specified time. Everything is wired in a specific manner and it would be most dangerous for you to ignore these orders!"

"Payment?" Bucky asked.

"That is as we had discussed. You will receive an envelope directly within thirty minutes after your assignment is complete. You will be taken care of, my friend." Slezak led him to the door. "Now, I still have much to do and your shenanigans with the telephone have created enough delay. I would suggest that you get some sleep on the train. You can't afford to be less than completely alert."

"I am looking forward to that envelope, Mr. Slezak. The thought of it will keep me very wide awake until it's in my hands." He picked up the doctor's bag and headed out across the grounds to the car. "Tomorrow, or should I say later today, is the big day," he thought to himself as he drove back to Princeton.

60

Alan Mowbray was not in his usual butler's uniform. Instead, he was wearing a navy pin-striped suit with a white shirt and black tie. He had just slid a pair of eggs out of the frying pan onto a gold-rimmed dinner plate. Crowded together with scones, Canadian bacon and a cup of black coffee, they traveled out of the kitchen on a serving tray held aloft by Mowbray. He knocked gently on the bedroom door. After a slight delay, the sleepy voice of Abigail Menjou seeped out. "Yes?"

"Good morning, Abby. I have breakfast for you. May I come in?"

"Yes, of course," she replied. He entered and set the tray on a table.

"If you don't mind," he said, and he went around the room pulling open the curtains on the large windows, causing the early morning light to come streaming in and making the still groggy woman squint her tired eyes.

"My gosh," she said, looking at her wristwatch, "it's only seven o'clock! What's the occasion for waking me so early? Oh, I'm sorry, Alan. It's just that last night I took some of those pills Dr. Ayres prescribed so I could get some sleep. I feel so terribly drained."

"I am extremely sorry to have to wake you at this ungodly hour, but I received the most urgent news last night after you had gone to bed."

"What is it, Alan?" she perked up, "Why didn't you wake me last night?"

"I received a phone call last night from Karl Krell. He was leaving to pick up another shipment but there has been an urgent development he wanted us to know about. First, though, Eve and Gordon are with him and they are safe. He also asked me to thank you again for playing the part of accuser so well during such a devastating emotional time. We all think you have been most courageous during this ordeal. Karl said he would clear up the details with Sergeant Gleason and you will suffer no repercussions for your statements."

Abigail dismissed the compliments, thinking the word urgent would apply to an issue of greater importance than pacifying her. "Please go on," she implored.

"He called to warn us about new developments concerning the informer. Apparently, the person who contacted Karl to tell him that someone knows about us has himself been killed. This implies greater danger for all of us. Additionally, uncovered on the body of the informer was a message that has been de-coded by Gordon and Eve which seems to lead to the World's Fair in New York City."

"What did he want us to do?"

"Karl did not give specific instructions except to say that we must be careful. If our group is known, as appears to be the case, none of us are safe." He went over and picked up the coffee cup and handed it to her. "I've been thinking about this all night, Abby. It seems to me that the danger to us is secondary to our mission."

She nodded in agreement. "I wouldn't want Adolph's life to have been sacrificed in vain."

"That's my thinking, too," he agreed. "Now, this might be like looking for a needle in a haystack, but it's my opinion that the breach of security in our group must be from within, and if something is planned for today at the New York World's Fair, then there may be a slim chance that the two of us can stop it."

Abigail looked puzzled.

"There will be thousands of people there – faces we have never seen or recognized. But, if we are there on the grounds watching, looking, just maybe we'll spot that one face of someone we recognize. Maybe a refugee that we carried through the dark to a new life. Maybe one of our inner circle. But their appearance at that location on a day we know has some nefarious meaning might be the only way we can solve this."

"But isn't that fair so huge?" she continued, "We couldn't possibly cover all of it ourselves."

"Of course not," he conceded, "but we have no chance at all of catching the fiend sitting here. If we are at the fair, who knows?"

She sipped the coffee and then pushed the tray away. She still felt a bit lightheaded. Depression, stress, the pills, not enough sleep. Maybe it was one or all of those things. She owed it to Adolph, though, and their mission to see this through. "You go get the car," she ordered. "I'll throw something on and I'll be out to join you in a jiffy."

She dressed quickly, grabbed a fork full of eggs and shoved the scone into her pocketbook. She tossed on her overcoat, the one with the fur collar, and slammed the bedroom door behind her.

Mowbray was in the driver's seat, the car humming. He leaned over to open the passenger door for her and then drove off toward their unknown mission in New York City.

61

It was almost like pushing a button. Pendleton shoved open the door shouting, "Chief!" and like clockwork, Gleason's feet fell off the desk and the Sergeant's eyes popped open. He had nodded off and slept through the night at his desk.

"Huh? Oh. Pendleton." Gleason quickly tried to regain his dignity. "I think you can drop that stake-out assignment at 26 Witherspoon."

"But, Chief…."

"No. No. I know you love sipping coffee for hours in the patrol car, but I got the inside dope that Gordon and Eve are locked up in Krell's office out in Plainsboro. So we'll look at some other leads."

"CHIEF!" Pendleton yelled. "I've got another lead already."

"Well, why didn't you say so. Spill the beans."

"I was watching the building last night when who do you think comes out but Bucky Carradine – way past midnight, too. I didn't think too much of it and so I just watched as he walked up toward Nassau Street. I really had to use the Boys Room by then – if you get my drift – what with all the coffee you'd been making me drink. So, anyway, I drive over to Pat O'Brien's bar. But, while I'm there, who do I see lurking around the back of the butcher shop but good old Bucky Carradine. He must've doubled back around so nobody would see him. Suspicious, I says to myself. So, I follow him. And where do you think he goes?" Pendleton paused. Finally Gleason realized that he was waiting for him to guess.

"I don't know. Timbuktu? Just tell me, Pendleton!"

"He goes out to that Bund Camp. Two in the morning, he's visiting a camp almost twenty miles out of town. Now, he's only in there about fifteen minutes before he comes out with one of them doctor bags."

"You sure there wasn't something else in that coffee besides coffee, Pendleton?" Gleason asked.

"No siree. Two sugars and a little milk, just a drop. I like my coffee dark…."

"Oh go ahead. What happened next?"

"Well, I follow him back to Princeton. He drops off the car right where he picked it up and then heads right back home. I think it's kind of crazy but I went back to watching number 26 and drinking coffee."

"That's it?" Gleason asked.

"Oh no. Like I said, I was drinking a cup of coffee and then maybe a half an hour later, who comes back out of number 26? Why, it's Bucky again, still holding the black bag. Well, he starts to go through the same routine again. Walks up the street, doubles back, gets the car. But this time, he drives to the train station. I hang around until I sees him get on the four o'clock local to Penn Station."

"New York, huh? At four o'clock in the morning? With a little black bag?"

"What's it mean, Chief?"

"I don't know. I just have a hunch. Something very funny is going on."

"Oh, I almost forgot, Chief. When he gets out of the car at the station and again when he gets on the train, he turns around to see if anybody's tailing him. I could tell he was trying to be nonchalant-like, but he did that thing where your head just sort of swivels around this way, then that way…" he attempted to give Gleason a demonstration.

"You know, the New York police are going to get tired of hearing from me, but I think I should probably give them a call," Gleason was half thinking out loud.

"Yeah. Tell them to look out for a tall skinny drunk carrying a black doctor bag. Geez, they'll lock YOU up!"

62

Gordon and Eve were both pacing in the small twenty-foot square office in which they promised Eve's dad they would remain – safe and sound, until he returned. They were going stir crazy, though, now that they knew the momentous pressure on her dad, Alan Mowbray and Abigail Menjou.

"We can assume that whoever killed the Professor must have also killed the informer," Gordon decided.

"Maybe it was Peter Lorre?" Eve offered. "He also threatened you and he seemed like the type that would enjoy the work."

"That's a definite possibility. We'll need to keep him in mind." There were too many unanswered questions, and they both agreed that being isolated in that little box would not help anyone solve anything...especially when they knew that something big was planned for that very day.

"Should we?" Eve asked Gordon.

"Let's make tracks!" he replied, grabbing her hand and heading for the stairs.

63

A dejected Edna May Oliver stood in front of the three-story brownstone on Flatbush Avenue in Brooklyn. A wooden sign nailed across the entrance told the complete story: "This building condemned. Construction on the new Vanderhof Office building coming this spring."

"Another dead end," Edna May thought. "It seems as though the forces of nature are determined to wipe out all traces of Alan Mowbray's past." With the Verdig Apartments, Mowbray's most recent residence on record, now vacant and about to be demolished, it seemed that her search had also been condemned to failure. She stood staring at the sign, trying to focus on what to do next, the loud noise of the occasional truck or car passing on the street interrupting her train of thought. She moved to sit on the brick stoop of the vacant structure when she could have sworn she heard a harmonica. It was faint, barely audible, but it was definitely a harmonica. And it was coming from inside the condemned building.

Pulling herself off of her seat, she found the entry door slightly ajar. As she pushed on the heavy squeaky door, the music grew even louder. More intrigued than hopeful, she entered the building and followed the sound up a massive wooden staircase, lit only by the daylight streaming in through assorted windows. At the second floor landing, she discovered a wide open door with the full sound of the harmonica and about a half-dozen out-of-sync voices echoing out into the corridor. She stepped into the doorway to find eight people all bouncing along to the music, all facing the far corner of the room.

"Excuse me," she said.

No one noticed her.

"A-HEM!" She loudly cleared her throat. Her feet began to tap involuntarily to the tune.

Still no one noticed. They were all busy singing "Polly Wolly Doodle all the day!" at the tops of their lungs. Edna May grabbed the door and slammed it shut with all her might. The music stopped and the crowd peeled aside so that the person who was the center of attention was now visible. There, sitting in a wheelchair with a harmonica up to his lips, was Lionel Barrymore. Square-jawed with long wisps of white hair accentuating his compassionate dark eyes, he did not seem the least bit annoyed at the interruption.

"Come in, come in. How may I help you?" he inquired of the new visitor.

"I am looking for anyone who may know a man named Alan Mowbray," Edna May said, getting right down to business. "I had been informed that he used to live in this apartment building."

"Hmmm," Barrymore mumbled, rubbing his chin with his visibly arthritic right hand, as if deep in thought, "and why are you looking for this man?"

"I am here," Edna May defensively replied, "under direction of Detective Sergeant James Gleason of the Princeton New Jersey Police."

"Well now, Miss...?"

"Miss Oliver."

"Miss Oliver, I think I might be able to assist you." He turned to the group that had been singing along to his harmonica. "I think we'll be done for now, but if you all want to come back this evening, we can try out a few new tunes."

"I'm sorry," Edna May cut in, "I didn't mean to break up…"

"No, no, no," Barrymore waved his hands, "I was getting a bit winded anyway." The group was filing out of the room. "Annie," Barrymore called, "can you bring that chair in the corner over here for Miss Oliver before you go?"

"Sure," the young woman replied. Then she propped herself up on her tippy-toes and spun like a top over to the corner of the room. She picked up a wooden kitchen chair and danced it over, placing it in front of Barrymore's wheelchair.

"Thank you very much," was all the puzzled newcomer could say as she plopped herself onto the chair.

Barrymore began to speak but quickly stopped as Edna May cut in. "Before you tell me anything, I just want to let you know that I, myself, am not at liberty to divulge exact details. I can only tell you that there was a recent murder in Princeton and the police suspect that other people might be in danger." Edna May's jaw was locked tight and her eyes narrowed to illustrate the earth-shattering seriousness of her inquiry.

"Well now, Miss Oliver, I'll try to help the best I can. I have, as a matter of fact, known Mr. Mowbray since, let's see, back in 1914. You see, I used to own these Verdig Apartments, named after my sweet mother's family, and I rented a room to him. He lived here until, let's see, it was 1934. No. It was '35. Yes, that's right. Spring of 1935. He moved out then. I haven't seen hide nor hair or him since."

"Mmmm. That does fit. Can you tell me anything about his character, friends, changes you may have noticed in him?"

"Well, let's see," Barrymore's demeanor became somber. "Most of the change came in the very beginning and then at the very end of his stay here. When he first moved in, he seemed quite normal. But he quickly began having some kind of problems at his job. You see, he was a salesman for the Brickter Salami Company. He was never much of a salesman, and this other guy, a guy named Henry Daniell – I remember his name because it was like two first names – he was stealing all of Mowbray's accounts right from under his nose." Barrymore stopped to explain how he had come by all this information. "You see," he chuckled, "there was a common telephone downstairs, right outside of my apartment, so, well, I kind of knew EVERYBODY's business." Barrymore looked off into the distance and shook his head. "The saddest thing, the one that probably broke the camel's back, was this one call from a reporter from the New York Times. They were doing a story on some rescue group that Mowbray was involved with…"

"I know about that group," she cut in, trying to get to

the facts, "please go on."

"Well, he was talking on the phone with this reporter for about five minutes, then he started shouting into the receiver and then a few seconds later, boom, he slammed the phone down so hard I thought he broke it. Now, my sister, Ethel – she was living with me at the time – she's a real kind lady, doesn't like to see anyone upset. She put down her knitting and went right out into the hallway and pulled him into our apartment before he could storm up the stairs. Well, my gosh, he was fuming. Apparently when he told the reporter what he did for a living, the reporter, dripping with sarcasm, said, and I remember Mowbray's words, 'So I can put in my article that your heroic group is made up of a professor of music, a doctor, a businessman, and…a salami salesman?' That's when he nearly broke the phone. Ethel tried to calm him down, but it was no good. He stormed out and we heard him stumbling in, drunk, maybe three in the morning. That went on for, oh, I don't know, maybe six months. Then, one day, he came home with a new acquaintance. A stocky man with red hair, very arrogant, what was his name? Ethel usually likes everybody no matter what their faults, but she said she just couldn't get used to this man. Something disturbing. Hmmm, what was his name? Let me see…."

He tapped lightly on his harmonica, thinking it might jog his memory. "Walter Slezak!" he blurted out. "That's it. Walter Slezak."

Edna May's eyes bulged open like an exotic fish. "Just as I thought," she declared unconvincingly.

Barrymore took her response in stride and continued. "From the time he met Slezak, Mowbray never came home drunk again. He became almost, shall we say, robotic. He took two jobs and seemed to work every hour of every day. Never relaxed. We never saw him spend a dime. At one point, he came to me and asked for a reduction in his rent. He mumbled something about a goal he had and how he needed to save every cent. Now, Ethel said – and she has a way with words – that sometimes embarrassment or failure can lead to anger and that sometimes anger can lead to determination. She said that's what she thinks happened to Mowbray. I asked her where determination led. That, she said, could be the problem." Barrymore ended the statement with added emphasis.

"And?" Edna May pleaded for the rest of the story, leaning forward now in the creaky chair.

"Well, that's almost all of it. He went on like that for almost 15 years, believe it or not, then during the crash, suddenly he was making more money than ever. Ethel said she thought he used all that money he saved to buy up all the good stocks, like J. Paul Getty did. But, we'll never know. Anyway, I think it was 1933, he and Slezak opened up a meat packing plant. Riley's it was called. Ethel said that we should never think the worst of people. She said that if he had saved up to go into business then he should be commended. But, when she tried to congratulate him one night, he went on this tirade about revenge and how his plans were starting to take shape. After that, we just stayed away from him. Then, one day in 1935, we noticed that we hadn't seen him for a couple of weeks. When we went up to his apartment, it was vacant. He had cleared out. Then we found out that he and Slezak had sold their business and that was that. That's all I know, Miss Oliver."

Edna May was already up from the chair. The word "revenge" reverberated in her ears, and she knew then and there that she needed to get in touch with Gleason.

"Does that phone you were mentioning still work?" she asked.

"Oh, I am sorry, Miss Oliver. All the power is gone in

this building. It's been condemned, you know. If me and my friends weren't squatting in the building they would have torn it down weeks ago. Darn bank forced us out so they could put up one of those fancy office buildings."

Edna May went over and shook his hand. "I don't mean to be rude, but I do have a murder to solve and another to prevent, so I have to get to a telephone. Let me just say that I thank you very much for your help." She headed toward the door. As she turned to say goodbye, she added, "As a former suffragette, I know you have a tough battle. But don't give up!"

The room was empty again except for Barrymore, who sat in his wheelchair, tapping on the harmonica trying to loosen the cobwebs in his mind. "That name…Edna May Oliver," he thought, "I'm going to have to ask Ethel when those suffragette marches were that we attended, and wasn't there one in Princeton?"

64

Edna May Oliver pursed her lips and puffed. The stray locks of hair that had come loose, dangling in front of her left eye were caught in that breeze and flipped back on top of her head. Momentarily. Then they just flopped right back down. I don't have time for this, she thought, opening up her valise-sized pocketbook and extracting a pair of scissors. She snipped off the swatch of hair and continued down the steps of the house she had just exited.

She had to get somewhere with a phone, and quickly. At the bottom of the steps she surveyed the neighborhood. She was among abandoned factories and deserted apartment houses and her chances of finding a telephone seemed slim to none. What she had discovered from the man in the wheelchair simply could not wait, so she hitched up her ankle-length skirt and did a fine imitation of running until she came huffing and puffing to a stop three blocks away.

It was a main cross street and showed the first signs of life for blocks. My God, she thought, my blood hasn't been pumping like this since back in the suffragette days. She pictured herself in the years leading up to the 1919 march through Philadelphia, holding big wooden picket signs: Women are People, too! She'd had plenty of splinters on her palms and calluses on her feet from those marches, but she was young back then and they had emerged victorious. That fighting spirit was back again now, and Edna May was determined to get to a telephone. A very tiny watch repair shop came into view and she hurried up to it. It was so small it would have required a shoehorn to squeeze two customers in at the same time. The sign announced, "Mischa Auer's Watch Repair and Sales." Underneath was the slogan, "If you've got an Auer, you've got the time." The door seemed to be stuck on a door jamb that had nailheads popping out every couple of inches. She pushed her shoulder into it and the door flew open, banged against the inside wall and set all the displays of watches and watch parts hanging on the wall into a frantic dance.

A man who was too tall for the ceiling crouched forward to greet her. "Dear lady, how may I help you?" His Russian accent was very pronounced.

"I need to use your telephone. I have to use your telephone this very minute." Edna May was nothing if not determined. "It's an emergency!"

"Ah! An emergency!" he turned to bring the phone

onto the counter for her to use. "The police? Do you want me to call the police for you, dear lady?"

"Well, yes," she wasn't sure how to say it was a long distance call she needed to place, "sort of."

"Sort of the police, or not sort of the police? What is the difference?" he asked, shrugging his large shoulders.

"It's Princeton," she blurted out. "I need to call the Princeton, New Jersey police department."

"Princeton?" he said in a surprised tone. "For what kind of emergency would you call the Princeton police department? Do you have any idea how long it would take for them to get here from there? Dear lady, are you sure you know what an emergency is?"

The spirit of the suffragette suddenly overcame her and flew right up into her vocal chords. "Just give me the phone, you ninny! I'll explain when I'm done."

Startled, he handed the telephone to her and slowly backed away while she dialed the operator. "Hello! Hello! I need to place an urgent call to Sergeant James Gleason of the Princeton, New Jersey police department. Hurry, please. It's an emergency!" There was a pause, then she said, "What! Not there? This is a matter of life and death! Where is he? What? Where? Oh, you don't say? Where in New York City? This is a big town, you know." She mumbled something to herself, then realized the dumbfounded Mischa Auer was staring at her. "They're checking for me…."

"Of course, dear lady," he replied, "who would not?"

"What? The World's Fair? You must be kidding me. What is he..on holiday? Well, listen, officer whoever you are. This is Edna May Oliver and if he calls in, you tell him I'm going to the Fair to find him. He'll know what it's about. Now, don't you forget or you won't have a job when I get back." She slammed down the phone. "Now, I need a cab. Where can I get a cab?"

Mischa Auer kept his distance and merely motioned out the window of his shop. She could see two men and a woman getting into a taxi. She rushed out the door, but then stuck her head back in for a second. "You know, if you hammer these nails into the frame you won't have such a problem getting the door open." Then she darted off across the street, her arm in the air to flag down a ride.

65

Nat Pendleton climbed the front porch and was ready to ring the doorbell. He stopped for a moment and made a note of the flower box on the front window sill. Right underneath was a pair of men's boots, thick with mud, and three big cans marked "white paint." He pulled out a small pad from his pocket, flipped up the cover and jotted down those details. These items were not here yesterday. They might not mean anything, but they might be a clue. He stuffed the pad back into his pocket and rang the doorbell. There was no answer. He rang it again, this time holding his thumb down on the button as if it would make the bell louder. Finally, the door swung open.

"Officer Pendleton calling, ma'am. Is Mrs. Menjou at home?"

"I wouldn't know, Officer," Margaret Dumont answered, "why don't you try ringing HER doorbell?"

Pendleton looked up at the number over the door, then to the left toward the Menjou's home. "Oh, uh. Beg your pardon, ma'am. My mistake." He backed off the porch. "They do look kind of similar."

"No. You're wrong. They don't." She closed the door

with a bang.

Pendleton started to walk across the front lawn, but stopped when he heard Mrs. Dumont come back onto the porch to call him back. "Officer? Officer?" she called. "Not that you have earned this information, but I just remembered something that may be of use to you."

"Yes, ma'am," he replied.

"Very early this morning I was out getting the milk off my porch and I saw Mr. Mowbray putting something in the trunk of the car and then he waited for Mrs. Menjou. I went over to say good morning and inquire about Abigail's condition, what with all that has happened. He informed me that they were driving to New York City. I was quite shocked by this trip," she gave Pendleton a knowing look, "but who am I to judge?" She went back into the house.

Pendleton scratched the back of his head as he returned to his patrol car. "What is this with everybody and their sister going to New York?"

66

"Are we there yet?" Gordon moaned.

Sergeant Gleason looked over his shoulder from the passenger side of the police car. "Look, Gordon. Stop being a pain in the neck. We're going as fast as we can. We'll get there when we get there."

"I told you we should have taken the train," he harassed Gleason some more. "Not only is it faster, it's much more comfortable. We could've even got up and stretched our legs."

"Oh, give it a break, Radits." Gleason was in no mood

for ribbing. As a twenty-five year veteran of the police force, James Gleason thought this time he really was putting his own job on the line. First, two calls to the New York police department that left him feeling like a jerk. Then this call from Eve Krell. Something bad is going to happen at the World's Fair, she says, and it's going to happen today. We can't leave it to the New York authorities to take care of, she says, we've got to go, too. And, does she listen when I say to stay put like she promised her father? No, of course not. She says if you won't take us there, we'll go ourselves. What choice did I have? Of course, I could have just said we'd take them and then have driven over to the jail and thrown them in the slammer. Any other time and that's what I might have done. Any other person, that's what I might have done. But, there's still that funny hunch about all of this. Too many clues pointing right to the World's Fair and to top it all off, Gordon and Eve were two smart cookies.

"So," he said, coming out of his daydreaming and turning back the couple sitting in the back seat, "when all this hubbub is over, the two of you getting hitched?"

"Wow. Isn't that the Lincoln Tunnel?" Eve pointed straight ahead.

"Sure is." Gordon affirmed.

"Eeeech." Gleason hated tunnels with a passion. He couldn't stand the smell, or the hollow sound as they drove through, or the eerie feeling of being closed in with walls on one side and the river on the other. He closed his eyes tight and didn't open them until he felt the popping in his ears, indicating that they'd safely exited the tunnel on the other side and his next sight would be the city.

As they raced down streets with tall buildings crowding both sides of them, Gordon broke the silence. "Why do you think they chose the World's Fair?"

"And why someone from Princeton?" Eve added.

"Right now, we just have to try to stop whoever it is from doing whatever it is they're planning to do," Gleason stated. "Later we can put all the pieces together."

"Maybe we have to figure it out in order to stop it," Eve suggested. "Look," she tried to string her thoughts together, "the only information, uh, this cryptic clue found on the dead man's body. You think he was involved with the German Bund, right? Maybe it's all related...anti-Semitic...anti-immigrant. Maybe?"

"Could be." Gordon added his thoughts, "But how would that tie in with the time capsule, unless it's related to Professor Einstein? One of the most well-known documents in the capsule is written by Einstein. He's Jewish. He's not a native of Germany, but that's where he immigrated from."

"Sounds logical," Eve agreed, "but how does that help us stop whatever is planned?"

The mundane blaring of horns accompanied them as they weaved through traffic, riding in silence toward the park, each of them desperately trying to put the pieces of the puzzle together in time.

67

Gordon and Eve rushed ahead of Gleason to the front entrance gates of the World's Fair. They had to stop at the fin-shaped risers, where tickets were duly checked. They turned to find the Sergeant talking with a uniformed attendant and seconds later, they were escorted into the park. A pair of futuristic-looking gold carts were waiting to whisk the group across the Avenue of

Transportation, once the busy Grand Central Parkway, toward the Trylon and Perisphere that towered over the central plaza. Waiting for them there was a group of New York City policemen and a couple of detectives. In the forefront, directing the group, was a short man with a refined British accent.

"Detective Claude Rains," he introduced himself. "And you must be…"

"Sergeant James Gleason," he replied, extending his outstretched hand. "Princeton Police Department."

"Ah yes," Rains remarked, "not enough going on in Princeton to keep you busy, Sergeant?"

"Well, to tell you the truth…." Gleason babbled.

"Just kidding you, Sergeant," Rains broke in. "We appreciate your tip and your help. I understand these two are the ones that figured out the code." Gordon and Eve introduced themselves and joined Gleason in telling Detective Rains all they knew. They were then escorted to the Westinghouse Pavilion where they were able to see the time capsule marker.

Rains had indeed taken the threat very seriously. There were security people in every possible position around and near the marker. It did not appear that any attack could have successfully been launched in the vicinity of the capsule. Rains had also assured them that bomb squads had searched the area to verify that nothing had already been planted. And, he added, more security would be arriving shortly to augment their normal coverage throughout the rest of the park.

"I think we have it covered quite extensively, wouldn't you agree, Sergeant Gleason?"

"Yup." Gleason nodded, and Eve and Gordon agreed.

Gleason turned to the couple. "Well, what more do

you think we can do here? This might have been a waste of our time."

Gordon and Eve had to admit that with the limited information they had, there really wasn't a lot more for them to do. "Do you mind if we just walk around a bit, Detective?" Gordon asked.

"No. No. Go right ahead," Rains replied. "I'd like to discuss a few things with Detective Sergeant Gleason anyway."

They walked off a bit, out of hearing but not the sight of Rains and Gleason. "Eve, we have to think. There has to be more to it than this."

Gordon was looking off into the distance, and Eve's gaze joined his. "I feel the same way," she agreed. "If we turn around and look at the capsule, it seems so simple. I mean, the capsule is supposed to represent civilization. Not be anything more important than that."

"Right." Gordon said. "The items in it are kind of like advertisements. There are products, pictures – nothing of real intrinsic value. It's a miniature vision or substitute for something else, the world of 1939." He continued, "So, oh my gosh! What if the message, the code on the paper was the same sort of thing? Like maybe it's their title or name for the bigger project?"

"Yes! I bet that's it! Think of the analogy Professor Einstein told you about going beyond the destination point or however you put it. If you look back, that point is still there. They named their project "40°44'" – whatever it is – because they thought not many people that would see that slip of paper would have a clue, as opposed to calling it, say, 'The 1939 World's Fair Bomb Plot' or some other name."

"Ahh," Gordon sighed. "You're not only gorgeous, you're brilliant!"

"Thanks," she blushed. "But where does that leave us?"

"I'm afraid that leaves us with the whole park to worry about."

68

Abigail Menjou was having difficulty keeping up with Alan Mowbray. They had been walking for close to thirty minutes, tracing the perimeter of the Pool of Peace and passing under the shadow of the huge copper-relief sculpture, "The Scholar, The Laborer and The Toiler of Soil." Abigail paused momentarily to take in the artwork but almost lost sight of Alan, who was intensely scanning the crowds.

At the Aquacade exhibit, the heel of her right shoe snapped and they paused for just a moment to survey the damage. Abigail asked Alan to break the heel on the other shoe and she continued on, hobbling through the park in two broken shoes. It slowed them down a little, but by this time the crowds were heavy and making headway was not easy anyway.

The awful smell from the herd of cows being milked in the Borden pavilion made her slightly sick to her stomach, but passing the aromas wafting from the Continental Baking exhibit and then the Wonder Bread building with its monstrous diorama greatly reminded her of her missed breakfast. At the Transportation pavilion, they were able to rise to an upper level deck that looked down over a wide area of the park. Thousands of fair goers were packed in the walkways below with barely enough space between them to even see the ground.

"This seems so hopeless, Alan," she said. "There are just so many faces that I can't distinguish one from another."

She thought he hadn't heard her, he was so intently searching through the crowd, and without turning to look at her he replied, "We cannot give up, my dear. We simply must keep going. For Adolph."

69

There was a commotion at the front gate. An elderly woman was batting the backs of two fair attendants with her orange and black umbrella. She refused to pay the admission fee and kept claiming that she was there to see a policeman from Princeton, New Jersey on urgent and important business. Within minutes of security guards being called to the scene, Edna May Oliver had been escorted through the gates and received the V.I.P golf cart ride to where Gleason and the others were waiting.

Edna May left the cart before it had stopped and her forward motion sent her straight into the arms of James Gleason. "I'm already married, you know, Edna May."

She pushed him away and started right in. "What are you doing in New York City? Don't you…."

"What are YOU doing here, Edna May?" he came back.

"Don't you remember? You sent me here to look up that information, you know, from the newspaper clipping Gordon and Eve called about?" She was speaking as if it were a secret between the two of them. Then she stopped, looked around and came to her senses. "We have to get back to Princeton. I know who the killer is and I think

Abigail Menjou's life is in danger."

"Calm down, Edna May," Gleason said. "She's safe and sound back in Princeton. Alan Mowbray is there to protect her and I've sent Pendleton over as extra backup."

"NO! That's the worst news you could tell me!" Edna May yelled back. "Alan Mowbray is the murderer!"

70

Gleason and Rains were off like a bolt of lightning as the golf cart sped to the nearest station in the park with a telephone.

In the meantime, Edna May told Gordon and Eve what she had uncovered.

"I'm sorry if I violated your trust, you two, but when you called me and told me about that torn bit of an article in the newspaper, I felt that I needed more help. I contacted Sergeant Gleason right away and he believed every word I said about the two of you. He sort of deputized me as an investigator and sent me off to New York to check the archives of the New York Times. I met an amazing woman archivist down in their vaults. Her name was Una Merkel. What being down in those dark corridors does to people! This woman had a mouth like an all-night diner – it never closed! Brilliant mind, though. I think she could recall every single article, every single ad in the Times by date, page and column."

Gordon broke in, "One day, there'll be machines that do that, at a push of a button. We won't have to count on the human memory."

Edna May looked at him as if to say, "I'm talking. Shut up."

She continued. "Una pulled out a one week pile of The Times and said she was sure it was in one of those. Wouldn't you know, it was the first one she handed to me. Same as the one you pulled out of the fireplace, except the year was missing from the article you found. Turns out it was from March 31, 1915. Well, the picture was correct. There were six people in the picture, including your father," she nodded toward Eve, "and Adolph Menjou and four others. What the text accompanying the picture revealed was that Alan Mowbray was the seventh member of the group, but he apparently never showed up for the ceremony and never gave an explanation as to why. I read the article word by word. I knew this was important in some way, but it was also a dead end. There was no further information about Mowbray. My only other recourse was to try and contact the families of anyone else in the group. I started to jot down the names when Una said that she had a thought. I'll tell you, that brain of hers really came in handy. She remembered Alan Mowbray's name from other articles.

"She traipsed up and down corridors for a few minutes and then came back with an issue of The Times from 1934. There it was in the business section. A small notice about the formation of a new company, Riley's Meat Packing Plant and the co-owners are listed as Walter Slezak of Third Avenue in Queens and Alan Mowbray of the Verdig Apartments in Brooklyn. Double gold, I thought. Who would even have guessed that these two men knew each other, let alone that they were partners in a business? I thought I was onto something and took a cab to the Riley Meat Packing Plant. That was a dead end. It seems that the two men had sold their interest in the plant a couple of years ago and they had both left town without any forwarding information. No one there even remembered Mowbray. My last hope was the Verdig Apartments and for that I ended up taking a bus that left me off six blocks from where the building was." Edna May then related the whole of her encounter with Lionel Barrymore. Edna May looked at them and concluded, "I am convinced Mowbray is behind the murders."

Just then, Gleason walked back toward them. "I just talked to Pendleton. According to their neighbor, Mrs. Dumont, Mowbray and Mrs. Menjou are somewhere in New York City."

"Sergeant," Gordon added, "I'd bet my bottom dollar that they're somewhere in this park."

71

The Nassau Inn sits on Palmer Square in the heart of Princeton. Only two years ago it had been rebuilt and that facelift, combined with its Revolutionary War era décor exuded aristocratic elegance. As Walter Slezak stepped into the Yankee Doodle tap room, he scoured the packed dining room. The clinking of glasses and plates permeated the room. A few of his customers from the butcher shop were in the process of finishing their meals, and Slezak made a point of greeting them as they exited the hall.

A maitre d' came over to where Slezak was standing and asked for his name. A reservation list was checked and then Slezak was shown to a corner table where his dinner partner was already seated. The man pushed away from the table and stood to greet Slezak. He was big and tall and his thick hand stretched out to vigorously shake Slezak's.

"I am Sig Ruman," the man said with a sharp

German accent, "and you are Walter Slezak, I assume."

"Yes, of course," Slezak said, pulling a handkerchief from his coat pocket and wiping the spray from his brow that had been spit out of Ruman's mouth. "It's a pleasure to meet you."

They both took their seats. Slezak told himself not to encourage Ruman to use any words that included the letter 'S'. "May I buy you a glass of wine?" Slezak offered.

"Why, that's most kind of you." Ruman leaned forward and in a hushed tone said, "we must remember to speak softly. Our meeting is of the utmost confidence."

"Yes, of course, Mr. Ruman. On that, I, too, agree."

Ruman then began the conversation. "If you notice, I have requested this table away from everyone else so that we may have the privacy we need. Meeting in my room, as I had originally suggested, would have given us much more of a guarantee of privacy."

"Ah, yes," Slezak conceded, "I agree. But, let me make this point, the actions that are being taken at this very moment will have a great deal to do with the successful business transaction we are engaging in. Our attendance at this table at this exact time in front of all the people in this dining facility offers both you and I the perfect alibi, if one is ever needed."

"Ah," Ruman said, tipping his straw hat to his dinner partner. "I am most grateful to have such a careful business associate."

"One can never be too careful, Herr Ruman."

"So, Mr. Slezak, will I be able to take possession of the goods tonight? I am most excited about this transaction. Most excited."

"As am I, Mr. Ruman. As am I." Slezak was practically bursting with pride. "Let me tell you, sir, I have taken the liberty of ordering for both of us the finest prime rib steaks they have in this establishment."

"I love prime rib," Ruman interjected.

"I provide it myself, through my other business venture, directly to their kitchen," Slezak beamed. He leaned in a bit and spoke in a lower voice, "The prime ribs are to be served to us in exactly thirty minutes. At that same time, synchronized perfectly, my associates will set off two bombs at the New York World's Fair. There are thousands of people there, my good man, and the chaos will be uncontrollable. It will be at that time of madness that a well-trained group of my men, disguised as workers at the fair, will enter the building known as the Masterpieces of Art. And, it is aptly named for it has all of the products that will make your mouth water, my dear business partner. Rembrandt, Da Vinci, Caravaggio, Michelangelo. Three hundred of them – priceless – or for your purposes, just the right price."

"A brilliant plan, my dear Slezak."

"Now, tell me. Does your mouth water more for the prime rib, or for the feast you shall receive this evening?"

"I am speechless, my good man, simply speechless." Sig Ruman then pushed his chair back and motioned for a waiter in the far corner of the room to come over. He pulled a cigar from out of his pocket and lit it over the candle burning in the center of the table. "You've never met me in person before, have you, Mr. Slezak?"

The color instantly drained from Slezak's face and he assumed a quite ghostly appearance.

"You see, my name is not Sig Ruman." His German accent had disappeared without a trace, replaced with a haughty British bite. "The name is Charles Coburn," he blew a puff of cigar smoke toward Slezak as he uncurled his fist to display his federal badge. "Government agent. Lock him up, John."

Slezak turned in horror to see the waiter, John "Bucky" Carradine, ready to clamp a pair of handcuffs over the butcher's wrists.

72

Charles Coburn quickly got on the phone to New York and passed all the information he had just obtained to the authorities on site in Flushing Meadows. Detective Rains and Sergeant Gleason acted swiftly to secure the Masterpieces of Art building. The truck parked near the galleries was discovered and the Bund members disguised as World's Fair workers were rounded up.

Bucky Carradine, who had exited the northbound train at the New Brunswick station and returned to Princeton, had obviously not carried through on his assignment from Walter Slezak to take a bomb and plant it at the fair, so there was now only one remaining threat.

Alan Mowbray.

Somewhere in the park it was now known that he had a bomb. He also had Abigail Menjou, and he was considered to be mentally unstable.

Police were under orders to treat him with extreme caution if they found him. And everyone was looking. Detective Rains had ordered the evacuation of the park, but they felt that from what Slezak had given as a time frame, there were now only minutes left.

Alan Mowbray looked at his watch. It was time to set the bomb. He reached the appointed spot on the second level of the ramp leading up to the Ford Motor Company exhibit. Across the way was the Futurama pavilion of General Motors and not ten feet above and right behind the ramp was the Tilt-A-Whirl ride zooming around and around. The plan had provided for the maximum amount of damage and chaos. When the bomb went off, it would collapse the ramp, the Tilt-A-Whirl behind it, and debris would rain down on the lines of people waiting for the Futurama below.

Mowbray stopped at what was supposed to be the optimum location. Abigail hoped he had spotted someone they recognized. "Alan? What is it? Do you see someone?"

As he looked down on the crowd, he could see that they were rapidly filing out toward the exits, the throng of people noticeably thinning out. He caught sight of two men in opposing spots some distance away looking straight at him, rifles pointed in his direction. It took his mind a split second to grasp the situation and then he quickly realized there was no turning back.

Abigail, still waiting for a response to her question, groaned as a gun was suddenly shoved into her back. "Alan! What are you…."

"Shut up! You might as well know this now. I killed your husband. He ruined my life and he paid for it. Just like the others. Professors, doctors, businessmen! They were there to help others but not me. As if I would ever have asked for their help."

No sound came from Abigail Menjou's moving, panicked lips. She was too terrified to speak.

"I have a bomb in this bag that was meant to kill you and many others, but it looks like right now, you and it are going to be my ticket out of here."

Sergeant Gleason was watching the scene from below. He could see the deranged Mowbray talking to a frozen Abigail Menjou. It was clear that any movement could end her life. Mowbray was pressed so close to her that sharpshooters could not take a chance. Then, without warning, something flew out of the Tilt-A-Whirl that was spinning by in the background.

It was Gordon.

He landed with a thud directly on Mowbray's back, sending both of them to a sudden impact on the cement surface. Mowbray's head crashed hard and left him unconscious. Gordon stayed there, pressed down on Mowbray, not taking any chances that he might move. Abigail Menjou collapsed in tears next to them. For what felt like hours, Gordon did not move. Finally he heard the scramble of feet coming at him from all directions and the next thing he knew Sergeant Gleason pulled him up. "It's okay, kid. He's not going anywhere."

Eve rushed over to hug him.

"And what was that all about, by the way?" Gleason demanded to know.

Gordon was still shaking from the impact, but he started to explain. "Well, we were up on the next level of the ramp when we saw what happened. We knew any movement and he would shoot Mrs. Menjou. Whatever happened had to be something too quick for him to react to it. We thought, why not the Tilt-A-Whirl? Eve figured the distance. Back at The Topic I had invented this lever thing to throw a football, so I just thought, why not a person? We used the Tilt-A-Whirl like a lever, she figured out when I should go and…."

"All right. All right. The math genius and the boy who can fly," Gleason said. "I think you need to go back to playing the piano," he said, pointing at Eve, "and you," he looked Gordon right in the eye, "you need to get back to the newspaper. Only I mean delivering them!"

73

The New York City police department treated the whole gang to a private car on the Pennsylvania Railroad, a luxury ride in style back home to Princeton.

Every one of them felt too tired to keep awake, but the end of the ordeal and the continuous supply of food being wheeled in kept them awake as they traveled south through northern New Jersey.

It was Sergeant Gleason who started to tie up the loose ends. "You know, Gordon, you sort of have Professor Einstein to thank for saving your life," he began.

"I don't get it," Gordon said.

"Well, didn't someone shoot at you in the canoe the other night?"

"Yeah. I almost forgot about that."

"Well, you know how Einstein likes to take walks along Lake Carnegie?"

"Sure."

"Well, the professor is a very notable person, and the government sort of watches out for him, if you know what I mean."

"Bodyguards?"

"Sort of," Gleason nodded. "There's a couple of men that basically follow him around, stay back a bit, but they are trained and ready to protect him."

"And…?"

"And when the professor was lost in thought walking along the lake the other night, his bodyguard happened to notice Peter Lorre taking a shot at you and preparing to take another. So, Mr. Kibbee put his bag of peanuts in his pocket, took out his gun, and took proper care of Mr.

Lorre."

Gleason continued. He explained that Mowbray had killed not only Menjou, but the informant in the alley. "As a trusted ally of Professor Menjou's group, he was above suspicion in the first murder. When he found out about an informer, though, he knew he had to stop him before he could do any damage. You see, Mowbray knew that the informant was a Bund member – not a member of Krell's group. He had to act to protect both his plot of revenge and his interests with Slezak and the Bund."

Edna May Oliver sputtered, "I don't think I've ever heard of such a thing in our area."

"The Bund isn't just a bunch of well-meaning Germans. It's been infiltrated by Nazis. They have a goal and they're filled with hatred - just like Gordon's article was going to show. Walter Slezak had been a part of that group for close to a decade, but when he and Mowbray became business partners, the news about Mowbray's old group reached Slezak's ears. The combination of Mowbray's need for revenge and Slezak's hatred of the Jews put Karl Krell's and Adolph Menjou's work and lives in jeopardy. The fact that a good man - a good German who mistakenly got involved with the Bund - came to his senses and tried to stop them ended up with him being killed in a back alley. But he didn't die for nothing. His clue, that one small scrap of paper in his pocket, eventually led to the foiling of their plots." Gleason's next statement caused Edna May to nearly topple out of her seat. "As a matter of fact, Bucky Carradine has been working undercover with federal agents on the Bund case for quite some time."

"Bucky? I mean, John?" Edna May gasped. "They trusted an alcoholic like that?"

"Just like perfume, Edna May. A dab of Scotch on the

lips, maybe a little on the tongue. A stagger here and a slur there. It all gives the right impression."

"My goodness," she said. "Bucky a federal investigator! I honestly can't believe that John was working with the Feds, I mean Federal agents, investigating this Bund thing. And to think I was almost certain that he was the one who clobbered Gordon in the hallway that night."

"I knew right away it wasn't him, Edna May," Gordon jumped in. "I was hit on the right side by someone taller than me. Bucky's taller than me all right, but his right shoulder has that injury from the war. The only other possibility was Allen Jenkins. Taller, right handed, lives one floor up from the incident."

"But why would he attack you?" Edna May asked.

"Nothing personal, I'm sure," Gordon offered. "He has a betting problem. Loves the horses. In fact, that's part of what convinced me. I sort of recall that distinct smell of horses right before everything went black. He just needed some money for the track, that's all. It just happened to be MY money."

Gleason broke in. "Gordon, you wouldn't have happened to mention to one Miss Spring Byington who you thought it was that clobbered you, did you?"

"As a matter of fact, Sergeant, I did mention it to her. How did you know?"

"Doesn't matter," Gleason waved it off. "Just explains a little incident down at the diner yesterday."

74

By the time the train rolled into the Princeton Junction station, the events of the day had taken their toll on the passengers in one particular car. Conversations had petered out and most eyes had lost their battle to stay open. The commotion on the platform caused by a shouting group of well-wishers quickly shook everyone out of their stupor. Karl and Kate Krell were at the forefront of the crowd and boarded the train as soon as it stopped. Kate and her daughter locked in a tight embrace as Karl firmly shook Gordon's hand.

"So, how are the relatives in Chicago, mom?" Eve teased her mother.

"I went to visit my cousin who is living in the Chicago jail. What's his name? Al Capone!" She chuckled at her own joke.

Karl further explained. "Your mother's ability to speak Russian and Yiddish is exceptional. She decided that hiding away while this unfortunate episode was unfolding would not be productive. So, she stayed with one of the families that had just arrived in the country and spent some time teaching them English."

"At least they can ask the grocer for a dozen of eggs and a pound of coffee!" Kate beamed.

"Excuse me, Mrs. Krell," Sergeant Gleason stepped in to interrupt. "I wanted to introduce you to a new acquaintance of mine. Well, he wanted me to introduce you to him. This is Charles Coburn," he turned and looked toward Coburn, "and this is Mr. and Mrs. Krell."

"A pleasure to meet you," Coburn said to Kate, clasping his hands around hers and giving a gentle smile. He turned to Karl and offered an outstretched hand. "And it is an honor and a privilege to meet you again, sir."

Karl looked up at this pronouncement and studied Coburn's face. It did not seem at all familiar. He shook Coburn's hand and stated apologetically, "I'm sorry, but you must be mistaken. I don't think I've had the honor of meeting you before…" His voice trailed off.

Coburn was expecting that reply and leaned in close to Karl. "Ah, yes. It was only one short meeting many, many years ago and it was quite dark, but I think you might remember telling me, quite sternly in fact, to 'shhhh.'"

To anyone observing Krell, it must have been obvious that a light bulb had suddenly gone off in his head. He grabbed Coburn's hand and shook it vigorously, as if he had just found a long-lost friend. "You certainly do get around, Mr. Coburn," Krell seemed to be in awe of the man, "and please accept my belated apologies for telling you to be quiet!"

"No offense taken," Coburn said. "Well, I must be going. I have a few things to clear up before I become, shall we say, a retired citizen of the world." Again he leaned in and whispered in Krell's ear, "and don't worry…I'll make sure that no one bothers you and the good work you're doing."

As he turned and walked off toward his car, he started softly singing a Robert Burns poem:

Should a body meet a body
Coming through the rye
Should a body kiss a body
Need a body cry?

As Karl turned back to Kate, humming the song to himself, her puzzled look prompted him to cease singing and start explaining.

"Remember that ship of German Jews that America turned back? The one that got our group back together? The night we were getting them off the ship, there was a crew member who was helping us to sneak the people off. He was tenderly singing that song while he was helping. I was afraid we would be found out, and told him to shush.

Well, the man explained that the men and women were anxious…terrified, and the children were on the verge of crying, so he started to sing this gentle lullaby to calm them down. It seems that it was Mr. Coburn who was our crooning cohort."

75

It was an hour later when the last of the group broke up at the station and headed home. Gordon and Eve were walking in front of the elder Krells.

"I'm famished," Gordon said, and looked back at Mrs. Krell, adding, "how about I come over and you cook up a batch of your rolled meat and cabbage?"

"The energy isn't in my bones tonight, Gordon. Maybe I will let Eve prepare it."

"Oh, no. Not that!" Gordon moaned. "I've already had my life in danger too many times in the last few days!"

Eve, a small but powerful girl, whacked him on the side of the head with a force equal to, if not greater than, the blow he received from Allen Jenkins.

76

"A thousand dollars in cash?" Grant Mitchell stared in disbelief at the bills strewn on his desk. "What in the world is it for?"

Charles Coburn replied, "Just a token of my appreciation. You run a fine newspaper, Mitchell. And I don't want my sister thinking I borrow money without repaying it"

"But, a thousand dollars?"

"Look, Mitchell. You might want to expand. Maybe hire a new employee, for example. Here's the cash to train them. Now I've got to go. You just sit down and count that cash. Make sure it's exactly a thousand. If not, just let me know."

"Sure. Sure," Mitchell replied, shaking his head and plopping down in front of the pile of ten dollar bills.

Coburn hurried out of the building, the bell above the door clanged as he exited. Mitchell began his count. Minutes later, when he ended at nine-hundred ninety, he yelled, "Miss Byington?"

There was no answer.

"Miss Byington!"

Charles Coburn's car, at that moment, was seen heading south, out of Princeton, with the former Miss Spring Byington in the passenger seat. Noisy tin cans tied to a "Just Married" sign banged along the road as the car disappeared into the night.

77

It was October 31, 1939. There was a distinct chill in the air and the moon was full over Lake Carnegie. A single canoe floated quietly out in the middle of the water, the moonlight shining on a young couple squeezed together in the middle of the boat. They had a big orange and black checkered blanket to keep them warm, but their teeth could still be heard chattering from the cold coming off the lake.

It was a full moon, though, and another crazy idea popped into Gordon's thick skull. He pushed off the blankets and stood up, the boat rocking back and forth. "Hopefully, I won't get shot this time."

"Oh, no," she laughed.

"Now, this time I mean it. I'm going to jump into this freezing cold water, probably get sick and die, unless you agree to marry me. Do you understand?"

"Yes," was all she said.

THE END

32567329R00104

Made in the USA
Middletown, DE
05 January 2019